The View from the Very Best House in Town

Meera Trehan

WALKER BOOKS

Text copyright © 2022 by Meera Trehan
Illustrations copyright © 2022 by Nicole Miles

First edition 2022

Library of Congress Catalog Card Number 2021943995
ISBN 978-1-5362-1924-1

LBM 26 25 24 23 22 21
10 9 8 7 6 5 4 3 2 1

Printed in Melrose Park, IL, USA

This book was typeset in ITC Usherwood.

Walker Books US
a division of
Candlewick Press
99 Dover Street
Somerville, Massachusetts 02144

www.walkerbooksus.com

A JUNIOR LIBRARY GUILD SELECTION

For my family

Asha

Sometimes it seems that Donnybrooke is everywhere.

You're not supposed to be able to see any part of Donnybrooke—the most amazing house Asha has ever set foot in—
from Sam's backyard. But from up in Sam's cherry tree, Asha
spots a speck, black against the blue sky. Donnybrooke's creepy
weather vane. It's the only bit of Donnybrooke she doesn't love,
assuming you don't include the people who live there.

"I can see Donnybrooke," she calls down to Sam, the fluttering
in her chest tight and familiar. She'd give anything to go back.

Sam doesn't reply. She can hear him, though, at the base of
the tree playing Househaunt on her phone, chasing down a pack
of buzzing, clicking monster-bugs.

"I can see it from here, Sam. Come up and look!" She catches
herself. Sam never climbs trees. "Actually, sorry, don't."

The phone lets out a few short zaps and a long sizzle. Sam must have killed off her infestation of Bed-Thugs. She'll thank him later.

"Sam, Donnybrooke—"

"You can't see that house from here."

"I can, for real," she says.

"No, you can't."

"I—" starts Asha, but this time the wind interrupts her, sending the cherry blossom petals around her in a swirl. Separated, they're so pale, they're almost white—it's like she's in a snow globe with her world being turned upside down. And just for that moment, Sam is right. Donnybrooke is gone.

Donnybrooke

aka The Grandest Mansion in Coreville and Possibly the World

First things first:

Of course Donnybrooke could see the girl. It's a basic law of nature: if she can see it, it can see her. And thanks to the wonderfully strong winds at the top of its hill, last week's storm cleared out a number of trees, not the least of which was one of those bloated oaks that had been practically breathing down its turrets. To be fair, that tree in particular was no worse than the rest of the poplars, pines, maples, and oaks that plague Donnybrooke, blocking the views of the finest residence in Coreville.

Donnybrooke couldn't see the boy she was talking to, though it heard him all too well. Ordinarily he'd hardly be worth mentioning in the same sentence as the girl, with her excellent architectural taste. But Donnybrooke has no choice

in light of the boy's egregious error. He referred to Donny-brooke as a . . . "house." *House?* As if Donnybrooke were built simply to be an ordinary shelter for an ordinary family?

The correct term is *MANSION*.

Two syllables even sweeter than the sound of the wood chipper gobbling up a fallen tree.

One last time: *MANSION*.

Ahhh!

Sam

"We should play soc-cer," says Sam as the petals settle on the ground. He says the last word like he might say *booger*, although Asha-soccer is the one kind of soccer he is willing to play.

As Asha climbs down the tree, Sam drags the goal back behind the azaleas, the best spot for hiding it. There's no way his mom can see it from inside the house or even the patio. That was Asha's idea, from years ago when his mom first decided that they should play soccer for at least thirty minutes of each playdate. One person would run around and kick while the other sat in the hidden goal pretending to be goalie, but really just spending the time thinking about whatever they wanted to think about. That was OK back then, but now that they have phones, goalie time is even better.

"You can be goalie first," says Asha. "My attic has At-ticks. But no At-tick Fana-tick, so it should be OK."

Sam takes her phone and runs to the goal. To make it fair, they have a rule that the goalie first has to help the person playing soccer with their Househaunt house, which means when Asha is goalie she builds extra wings and levels on Sam's house because that part is boring and hard for everyone except Asha. When Sam is goalie, he fights Asha's monsters because she hates fighting, especially bloodsuckers as big as her avatar. Of course that's the best part of the game, but whatever, more fun for him.

He enters her Househaunt house and grabs a flaming torch from the stairway that leads up to the attic. Then he swings open the door. Sure enough, a troop of human-size ticks is ready to clamp onto him and suck. A few even try. But as soon as he points the torch at them, they retreat, and he backs them up toward an open window. One by one, they scurry out. Mission accomplished. If only the At-tick Fana-tick were so easy to defeat . . .

"Sam! Sam!"

His mom is out on the patio, yelling. At him. Sam drops Asha's phone and bolts. His mom must have found them out. He searches his brain for some excuse that will let him avoid a lecture on how practicing soccer is for his own good, but before he can come up with anything, he's at the back door.

"Come inside!" says his mom, her voice a little softer.

He does as she says, and she shuts the door behind them. Then she throws her arms around him, squeezing hard, and says, "We did it, Sam! We did it!"

As Sam frees himself from her grip, he realizes two things: Whatever his mom is talking about, it's not soccer. And she is not mad. In fact, she's the opposite.

"You got into Castleton, Sam! Castleton! And to think I was so worried. But you're in!"

Sam's chest tightens and lightens like a star is being born right inside it, like all the stress inside him is making something new and bright. Miraculous even, if you believed in miracles. Because Castleton Academy has picked him.

It's not just that it's the best school in town. It's not just that it's really hard to get into. It has its own planetarium. And its own flag with the Castleton coat of arms . . . and did he mention its own *planetarium*! He and Asha used to go on field trips there, and he'd see the kids with their green polo shirts lining up in the halls and wonder what it would be like to have Castleton decide you were good enough to be there every single day. Now he, Samuel J. Moss, is going to find out.

His mom is talking faster now and not entirely making sense. "We knew you could be Castleton material, but I'm just thrilled they saw it, too! You're such a smart kid, but still—it's very competitive, and with your challenges—"

Challenges? For a split second, the star feeling in Sam's chest dims, but then his mom says, "Anyway, none of that matters now because you're going there! After all our work, you're going! Do you realize how amazing this makes you?"

Being amazing isn't really the kind of thing that can be measured, nor is the awesomeness of being selected by a school with its own planetarium, but in this moment, Sam doesn't care. He's amazing, it's going to be awesome, and that's enough.

"Oh, Sammy. Let me show you the acceptance letter so you can see for yourself. It's up on my computer. This is going to open so many doors for you!"

Sam takes a look out the window before following his mom upstairs to the study. Asha's back in her tree, on the outside looking in.

Asha

Sam is gone a long time, long enough for Asha to get her phone, see that her house still has a few At-ticks, climb back up the cherry tree, and study the petals that have bunched in the crooks of its branches. She wishes that they actually were snow-flakes; watching snow melt would be better than being stuck in a tree wondering when Sam will come back. She presses on the pattern in the wood where a branch was cut away, her finger-print to the tree's. Finally she texts her big brother, Rohan, even though she's trying not to bug him all the time because he's at college, and her parents keep telling her that college is busy.

Sam went inside. And he's not coming back.

Nothing. Rohan is probably busy writing a paper or working on some computer project or doing whatever it is you do when there's only three and a half weeks left in the spring semester.

A message pops back up: **Time waits for no man.**

Argh! He's in one of his scholarly moods. He's probably rubbing that stupid, stubbly beard he's trying to grow as he types.

Stop it! she responds.

Sorry. ☺ Give it a few more minutes.

She knows Rohan is trying to be helpful, but he doesn't understand how long Sam's been gone. Should she walk home? It's kind of far, but she's done it before. She could text her mom or dad to come get her, but then they'll want to know what is wrong, and nothing is wrong, except that Sam isn't coming back out.

Asha takes one last look in the direction of Donnybrooke. Yes, it's definitely the weather vane. She can imagine the rest: the deck, so high up that it's almost as if you're looking at a 3D map of the town below. And along the roof and sides, skylights and windows of all shapes—round, oval, arched, square, and rectangular, narrow and wide. And inside, columns galore, some topped with scrolls, others with leaves, and a few with nothing at all. Most of the houses in town are just what you'd expect—ramblers with galley kitchens and first-floor master bedrooms; center-hall colonials with formal dining rooms and symmetric windows; split-levels, like her own, with short staircases and basement rec rooms. She likes them fine, of course—she likes all houses—but they're nothing compared to Donnybrooke. She wonders how it would feel today, if it had feelings. Would it be celebrating that it was spring? Or, like her, would it be nervous about something?

Asha lowers herself down the tree. She squints at the back windows of Sam's house but can't see anyone. She runs to the patio door and knocks.

There's no reply. She knocks again, louder this time, and then forces herself to turn around, take five steps, and count to ten before knocking again. Before she finishes, the screen door creaks.

Sam's back. He steps toward her, then away, then toward her again. Butterflies move like that, in starts and stops, and Asha remembers why they used to scare her when she was little.

"What's wrong?" she asks before he gets too close.

He walks to the soccer ball and kicks it hard enough that it bounces off his fence.

"What's wrong?" she asks again.

"Nothing is wrong," he replies, and runs over to where the ball landed.

"You're playing soccer. What's wrong?"

"I'm not. I just kicked the ball once. And I'm happy. That's it."

Sam sounds like her mom when she wants to keep a secret. Asha tries again. "I think my next Househaunt house might sort of look like Donnybrooke. If your game is set to difficult mode, there's a house you can pick that has turrets, but also dormer windows . . ." She knows she's told him this before, but at least she's not asking him about the secret he's trying to keep, so he ought to appreciate it. "They both have spiral staircases, but in Donnybrooke it's in the back and in the Househaunt one I think it's in the front. There's also—"

"I'm going to go to Castleton Academy." Sam's voice is proud and stiff, like a pair of new dress shoes.

"What?!"

"Castleton Academy." This time he says it slowly, like it's the name of a foreign country he's reading off a map for the first time. Then he speeds up. "That's why my mom called me in. Because she just found out I was accepted. And I'm going to go."

"No!" Asha knows sometimes she hears things wrong. This has to be one of those times. "You're not."

"Yeah, I am. And it's the best school in Coreville. And it's got that planetarium!" Sam adds, which obviously Asha knows since they've attended three field trips there over the past five years and sat next to each other each time they watched a demonstration of what the sky over Coreville would look like that night.

"You can't go there." Asha's face is hot, and her head is muddled like when she's played too much Househaunt in the car. She shouldn't even have to say this. It's not just that he's her best friend, or her one friend in middle school, or the friend she's had the longest. It's not just that he keeps her from being alone now that Rohan's off at college. It's that they're the same. And they're different from other kids, especially Castleton kids. She knows this the way she knows the tilt of her roof or the layout of her room.

"Why can't I go there?" says Sam, sounding like Sam again.

Asha bites her lip hard. Does he really not know? Her parents have drilled into her that she's not supposed to ask other kids about their diagnoses or differences, not even Sam, but surely he's autistic like her, right? They spent five years in speech together. They get each other. She's never needed to ask out loud because the answer was obvious. But at this moment she wonders if she was wrong. Or if she's somehow fallen behind.

"Why not?" he asks again.

How can Asha explain this to him without saying what she's not supposed to? She looks up to the sky. Clouds are gathering in the direction of Donnybrooke.

"Prestyn goes there," Asha finally says. The one girl lucky enough to live in that amazing house and mean enough to keep Asha out.

"So what?"

How can Sam say that? Asha has told him all about Prestyn at least a hundred times. About how awful she was that one time Asha visited Donnybrooke and how none of the neighborhood girls would play with Asha afterward. About how Prestyn and her friends used to giggle whenever they saw Asha at the park or the pool or on a planetarium field trip, and when Asha would ask why, they'd just laugh louder. About how now Prestyn ignores her, but in a way that feels even worse than the laughing ever did. "I'm talking about Prestyn *Donaldson*."

"I know. You always talk about her."

"She's Prestyn the—"

"I don't care about her or her house."

What is going on with Sam? He doesn't even finish their joke. It's like he's pulling away on purpose. Asha is flooded with the urge to yank him back and shake him until he understands.

"We're not like her. We're not." She points at him hard and accidentally pokes his chest. She instantly regrets it. But before she can apologize, Sam picks up the soccer ball and runs back inside his house.

"You're wrong! And I'm going to Castleton just like her," he calls before the wind slams the door shut behind him.

More petals swirl through the air, clouding Asha's view. Her world is spinning again, but this time she doesn't feel like she's in a snow globe. She just feels sick.

Donnybrooke the Mansion

That Simply Requests That You Use the Proper Terminology

To be clear, the boy is as similar to Prestyn as a simple rambler is to Donnybrooke. In fairness, no child can truly compare to her, just like no other home can compare to Donnybrooke. That's the whole point of being the best. You're in a class by yourself.

And again, Donnybrooke is a MANSION. If you must call it a house, then, like Mrs. Donaldson, please be sure to affix the term *dream* beforehand, as in *dream house*.

Sam

Now that it's the end of August, Sam can say for sure: this has been a seriously weird summer. Even though he was smart enough to get into Castleton in the first place, his mom made him get tutoring in reading comprehension and writing, which he hadn't needed in two years. She kept taking him shopping for uniform clothes: one trip for the green polos, V-neck sweaters, and blazers with the school coat of arms on the chest, and then four more for khaki shorts and pants that were "stylish enough for Castleton," according to his mom, but also comfortable enough for Sam to make it through the day. And his mom made him get his hair cut twice—three times if you count from when he got the acceptance last spring. His mom even tried to sign him up for soccer camp so he'd be ready for the after-school soccer club, but thankfully, it conflicted with his tutoring. Instead his mom had him start running for exercise, which he worried would feel just like soccer but without the ball and other kids. But maybe even soccer wouldn't feel like soccer without that stuff because the running is just fine.

And then, in August, he took a vacation that was more than fine. The best ever, actually. For his birthday, his parents took him to visit not one, not two, not three, but four different planetariums, including the Hayden Planetarium in New York City. Every time the stars appeared on the domed ceiling above him, his chest filled with the joy that comes from sitting under a shelter that can display the visible universe. Every movie he watched reminded him that the true heroes in space aren't just the astronauts, but also the physicists and engineers who do all the work behind the scenes. Work he can do one day, especially now that he's going to such a good school. At the Hayden Planetarium, Sam even met an astrophysicist with a comet named after him. The whole drive home, Sam thought about what it would be like to have an object with your name whizzing through space.

The whole thing was pretty weird for a family vacation, but good weird. His parents were happier than ever and talked with him about every space fact and never made him feel like he should be thinking of something else. It was awesome-weird, actually.

The weirdest summer thing of all, though, was yesterday when that reporter from the *Coreville Gazette* came over. At first, Sam thought it was pretty cool that someone wanted to write an article about him—his mom told him that not many kids his age were featured in the newspaper. But then the reporter lady came in wearing these enormous earrings that looked like a model of the solar system if you thought all the planets' orbits were circular and had no sense of scale. She only talked to his mom, like he wasn't even there, asking all sorts of questions about what Sam was like when he was little, and his mom started crying and saying, "Happy tears, happy tears," which was really awkward, so he went upstairs halfway through to play Househaunt on his phone.

But today his mom has left for a weekend away with some of her mom friends, and Sam is ready for a normal day. His dad has taken him to the park—his dad always takes him to the park when his mom is away, no matter how many times Sam says he's fine just staying at home—but at least his dad doesn't bug him to play soccer. He lets Sam do what Sam wants, and Sam lets his dad do what he wants, which is to get out his phone and check his email. Sam's dad likes his email as much as Sam likes space. Maybe more, actually.

They get out of the car, and Sam starts running on the path that leads toward the playground and tennis courts, and away from the soccer fields. He hits his stride quickly, and his footsteps fall into a satisfying beat. He's so focused on his rhythm that he's almost at the swings when he realizes he's a few feet away from someone he knows.

Asha.

Her back is to him, her long black ponytail flying out behind her as she swings high, not letting her feet skim the ground. He goes still. He hasn't seen her since the last day of school, when she apologized for saying he didn't belong at Castleton. That was two months ago—it's probably their longest time apart since they met. He did ask his mom about seeing her a few times, but she always said they had too much to do or Asha had activities or relatives in town, and besides, he'd be meeting Castleton kids once school started. It was a little weird because usually his mom made sure he had plans with Asha every couple of weeks, but it's also true that this summer, getting ready for Castleton, has felt busier than any summer he can remember.

Asha's feet crunch to a stop, and she spins around in her swing.

"Sam!" she says cheerily, like she just saw him last week. Whatever weirdness there was about Castleton is gone.

He plops down next to her. "Hi, Asha."

"Have you been under your planetarium umbrella much?"

Sam grins. "A few times." Asha gave him the planetarium umbrella as a present three birthdays ago. He was a little confused when he unwrapped it and found a boring black umbrella large enough to shelter his whole family. But then he popped it open and understood. She'd decorated the inside with drops of glow-in-the-dark paint, and she'd clearly followed a star map of the Northern Hemisphere because all the constellations lined up just as they might in real life. It's true that it's not the same as the real planetariums his parents took him to, but it's also true that you can't keep a real planetarium in your bedroom closet to go under whenever you choose.

"Are you nervous about school starting?" he blurts. "Do you feel ready?"

"I'm always nervous to start school. Always."

"But we were at Sullivan last year. It's not even going to be new for you."

"Every year is different and you don't know how it's going to be different until you're in it. So, I'm nervous." She turns around and around in her swing so the chains crisscross.

"Yeah, I am, too," says Sam as she spins herself out. It's a relief to admit it out loud.

Asha reaches in her pocket and pulls out her phone. "Do you want to trade?" she asks.

Within seconds, they've opened up each other's Househaunt houses. They're both at the point where they're trying to design the inside of their houses. They have to be careful because in this game every time you make a mistake—say, put in a room that has sunlight shining down from the ceiling in a house with no sky-lights—you sprout monster-bugs. The bigger your mistake, the mightier the monsters.

After you finish your original house, you can put on additions with more and more rooms. It's not just that having a big house is cool; it's also that each room contains hidden weapons to add to your arsenal—like salt cartons or silver knives—heck, even sky-lights can come in handy when you're fighting off Vampire-Chefs on a sunny day. Asha once built Sam a basement laundry room, which might sound boring, but it not only fried Bed-Thugs in the dryer, it also connected to a laundry chute, which was a very use-ful escape route.

Asha basically never makes design mistakes, so she would never need him if that's all there were to Househaunt. But it's not. Once you build your house, you have to maintain it and keep it clean. Just like a real house collects all sorts of dirt and dust, a Househaunt house collects all sorts of monster-bugs, and the longer you wait, the worse they get. Rohan says that's actually just the game makers' way of making sure you play more often, which is kind of evil but also pretty smart. Anyway, Sam is glad they built the game that way because it gives him something to be good at, too. In fact, Rohan told him he was "a monster-killing genius" when he first taught them how to play, and it is kind of true. So far, Sam has been able to beat every kind of monster except the At-tick Fana-tick. Even Rohan, who has been playing for years longer, can't kill it.

"Do you want a finished attic?" says Asha. "I'll be really careful."

The risk with an attic is that if you mess up badly enough, it can sprout the At-tick Fana-tick. Everyone hates it because it's one of the only ways you lose your entire house and all your lives and have to start over. Basically, it's as bad as having your house condemned. But for Sam, it's even worse because sometimes when you're fighting the At-tick Fana-tick, it takes you up on top of the roof, spins you around until you're a blur, and flings you through the air. It's like it's designed to remind Sam of how much he hates heights. And who wants to be reminded of their worst fear? No one, that's who.

But as he investigates the perfectly designed attic in Asha's house and finds a set of fire extinguishers, he reconsiders. Finished attics always have the most unusual weapons hidden in them, and Asha would build his flawlessly. And that could buy him extra time to figure out how to defeat the At-tick Fana-tick once and for all—and get the extra lives and everything else that goes along with that. As he weighs the risks, he spots of a couple of Screech-Leeches in Asha's pipes. While he searches for a box of salt, an icky shape-shifting bug called a Witch-One emerges from the vents. Luckily Sam is next to a fire extinguisher, which he unloads on it. Asha glances over.

"Ooo—nice!" she squeals as the Witch-One evaporates.

Sam grins. It was a nice move, and it gives him time to find the salt, fill up the fire extinguisher with it, and give a Leech a solid blast. As it shrivels with a screech and a slurp, Sam realizes that sitting here in the sun with Asha, playing their favorite game, he's having the best time he's had all summer, aside from his trip to the planetariums. As Sam reloads with more salt, his dad's blindingly white sneakers stop in front of the swings.

"Well, hello there, Asha," he says. "I hope you've had a nice summer."

"I have, thank you."

Sam kills the other Screech-Leech and thinks a little more about the finished attic. He's leaning toward having her build it. Asha's attic makes her house way cooler and more powerful than his.

"Sam, it looks like there's a surprise for you!" says his dad.

Sam stiffens in his swing. He's not a fan of surprises.

"Your mom just forwarded me an email. You have a party tonight!"

"Party!" says Asha.

"Party?" says Sam. Who invited him to a party?

Sam's dad leans back, squints at the screen, and reads, "'The incoming seventh grade class of Castleton Academy is invited to a footloose and fancy-free evening to kick off the school year. Please join us at seven p.m.' There's a note from the host apologizing for sending this so late. She just got our email address."

A Castleton party. Tonight. He feels his insides shrink like the Screech-Leech he just decimated.

"You said we'd go to Fastburger for dinner," says Sam.

"We can go beforehand," says his dad. "Mom wants you to go to this thing."

Sam's mom loves parties. He remembers his mom taking him to his neighbor Connor's indoor soccer birthday parties at the Coreville Sportsplex. He was invited twice, and both years tried to wait it out in the hall, even though it smelled like dirty socks and snack bar grease. His mom wouldn't let him leave before the cake was cut.

Sam turns away from his dad, and the chains of his swing lock together. He knows this party won't involve soccer or any other sport, but he still doesn't want to go. It was not in the plan. And it's with Castleton kids. It's not that he hasn't met anyone there. Before he got in, he had an admissions visit where he sat in a class with half the kids in his grade, and even saw a show in the planetarium with them. He doesn't need to go tonight.

"Look, Sam," says his dad, sounding too cheerful, "it says, 'Please feel free to bring a guest.' You can bring Asha."

"Really?" asks Asha.

"If it's OK with your parents," says Sam's dad before Sam can answer.

"They're at a wedding out of town. Rohan's in charge." She pops out of her swing and runs toward the tennis courts.

"Rohan's here?" exclaims Sam, following her. Sam doesn't want to go to this party, but he does want to see Rohan. Rohan who taught him Househaunt and talks to him about astronomy and who he hasn't seen since last summer. Sam has always thought life would be so much easier if he had a big brother like Rohan to show him the ropes.

When Sam gets to the tennis court fence, Asha is already talking to Rohan, who is not quite as tall as Sam remembers and, it appears, is trying to grow a beard. Rohan rubs his fuzzy chin. The first thing Sam hears him say is, "Socialization is a critical activity across species."

Sam has no idea what that means.

Apparently neither does Asha. "Rohan! I told you to stop talking like that."

"You can go to the party if Sam's dad can drive."

"Yes!" Asha jumps up and down.

To Sam's surprise, the knot in his stomach loosens. Maybe with Asha there, it'll be kind of like it is here at the park except inside. Maybe he won't have to try to fit in with the other kids or wonder whether he's really Castleton material. Maybe the two of them can find a quiet corner and play Househaunt. Maybe she'll build him that attic and he'll fight off her monsters and together they'll ignore the rest of the party. That could be fun.

Rohan grins at Sam and puts his hand to the fence for a high five. "You ready for a party, Sam, my friend?"

Sam presses his hand against Rohan's and nods. He hopes he is.

Because ready or not, it's coming.

Donnybrooke the Mansion

and the Most Sought-After Site for a Party in Coreville

This evening's festivities will be hosted by Donny-brooke, the extraordinary residence of the Donaldson family: Mr. Dexter Andrews Donaldson, Mrs. Brooke Allen Donaldson, and their lovely daughter, Prestyn Arabella Donaldson. Mr. Donaldson, who considers himself something of an expert in architecture, as well as most other things, likes to say, "The most important thing about a house is what it communicates to the outside world." And everything about Donnybrooke says it's the best. As the largest home sitting at the highest point in Coreville, it has three chimneys, four turrets, a five-car garage, ten types of windows, a swimming pool, an elevator, a roof deck, and wrought iron gates decorated with a one-of-a-kind D&B crest, and it is surrounded by enough trees to keep a paper mill going for a decade.

In the interest of full disclosure, were you to look at Donnybrooke's deed, you would find that it's technically called 10001 Hunt Place, though you'd have to be coarse as a weed to call it *that*. And it doesn't actually have a brook running through it. Rather, it was named after its refined owners, who recognized its uniqueness by naming it after themselves even before the marble was put down in the foyer. After all, it's the family that makes the mansion, and the mansion that makes the family. Together, they're in a class by themselves.

Admittedly, at times, being the best can be a touch lonely. But there's nothing like some festivities to make it all worthwhile. The kind of party where fairy lights are strung along the roof deck, counters are heavy with bowls of fizzy punch and platters of endless snacks, and a temporary dance floor and disco ball grace the living room. The kind of party where the rooms overflow with guests who drip with awe and jealousy. The kind of party that makes Donnybrooke feel even more loved than all the ordinary homes in town put together. It's been too long since that's happened.

Too long for the Donaldsons, too. And they could undoubtedly use the boost as much as their mansion. These days, they're out of sync: Mr. Donaldson has more excuses to be away, Mrs. Donaldson hasn't been herself, and Prestyn hardly talks to either of them. Donnybrooke has seen what can happen to houses when their families fall apart: they're sold to *an entirely different family*. And the house is never quite the same after that. But that's not going to happen here, not now. Because the Donaldsons are about to have a night to remind them of who they've always been and must always be: the finest family in the finest home in Coreville.

To think Prestyn made such a fuss about having this party in the first place, saying she was sick of everyone—her classmates, her friends, her parents (please note, her mansion was not on the list). Mrs. Donaldson intervened with some of her classic pearls of wisdom: "You don't have a party because you want to be with them, you have a party so they'll want to be with you" and "Just because you're pretty doesn't mean you get to stop trying." When that didn't work, she switched tacks: "I wish I'd been lucky enough to have a mom who wanted to throw me parties like this." But Prestyn didn't budge one bit until Mrs. Donaldson finally said, "Fine, if you want to be like Asha Wood down the hill, I can't help you."

Such a perplexing statement in light of Asha's excellent architectural taste. Her awe when she looks at Donnybrooke or speaks of it—it's clear she appreciates the mansion more than anyone else, even when it's not dressed to impress. But perhaps Mrs. Donaldson is still a bit sore from that last time she was over, all those years ago. Anyway, what's important

is that the party is happening: Prestyn relented, Mr. Donaldson cleared his schedule, and Mrs. Donaldson sent out the invites. And now they'll all remember how much they need one another. And how much they need their dream house. It's going to be perfect.

But wait! Who's this coming up the drive? Is she finally allowed back? It has been too long since she's visited. Far too long. And yet Donnybrooke didn't hear a single word about her coming. Quite the opposite. Surely it would know if the Donaldsons were expecting *her*.

Oh, dear. This could put a wrench in the works.

Asha

Asha didn't know the party was at Donnybrooke. Really she didn't! She'd only been in the car for a minute when Sam's dad turned onto Hunt Place, and yes, maybe then the inside of her chest got a strange tingle, as if a creature were trapped and fluttering, because how could you not suspect when you're on the street that ends at the Donnybrooke gates? But she didn't know for sure until now. She hadn't planned to show up.

Her parents would be so mad if they knew she was here. They've told her she shouldn't even *think* about Donnybrooke as much as she does. But how can she ignore it when it peers over her house, the edge of its property skirting her backyard? She's loved it since it was just beams and rafters peeking over the tree-tops like ribbons on a birthday gift. She dreamed of going inside before there even was an inside to go in.

And though it's been six years—over two thousand days!—since her first visit, she's never again seen light and space quite like that, not in any of her architecture books and magazines. Being in the entryway was like standing at the bottom of a light-filled ocean, the enormous crystal chandelier greeting her like a shimmering upside-down giant squid. And farther in, it was like exploring an almost magical forest, except the columns were the trees, casting long shadows, making pathways of light and dark. Around every corner, behind every doorway, was some sort of delightful surprise—a diamond-shaped window, an archway as high as three of her, a ceiling shaped like the inside of an ice-cream cone—she never knew what she'd find next. She's been dying to return ever since.

And now, all of a sudden, she's back, in Sam's car, driving through the gates. The sun is low, shining straight on the house, turning the pale facade bright gold and the charcoal turrets black as witches' hats. She's too close now to see the weather vane, but she knows it's there—the eagle mid-flight, ready to pounce on the fish. Her heart is pounding. She forces herself to take five rose-and-candle breaths—in through her nose like she's smelling a rose, out through her mouth like she's blowing out a candle—just like Dr. Wells taught her. It only kind of works, and she takes five more.

She should say something. She should definitely say

something. But what? She *is* allowed to be here—they invited Sam and a guest, and she's the guest. And she wants to be here. Through the driver-side window, Sam's dad is shaking hands with a man in a green baseball hat with a large embossed *S*. That must be Prestyn's dad. Asha can feel her cheeks stretch too wide, and she wants to stress-laugh, except that she doesn't. Not here.

As she hears the clack of Sam's car door opening, she takes another deep breath and presses her fingertips together. Before she can open her door, Prestyn's dad does it for her, and the heat from outside rushes in. She needs to say something normal, something present, though as she takes her first breath of Donnybrooke air, it's hard to think what that might be.

She makes herself look right at Prestyn's dad. "What does the *S* stand for?"

Prestyn's dad taps his hat and smiles. "The Stonebury School. I went there from seventh to twelfth grade, if you can believe it. It's where I graduated high school."

His hat is from his high school? "That must have been decades ago."

Prestyn's dad laughs. "It was. But I really liked that school. Still do." He motions her and Sam forward. "Ready for a little chaos?"

Asha steps forward, her flat sandals slightly slippery on the marble stairs. The noises of the party are drifting down, and she can picture the long second-floor balcony, the atrium window that was bigger than she was the last time she visited. A small part of her knows that it's not too late to leave. She lives so close, Sam's dad could drive her or she could even walk. She'd be home in minutes.

But then she might never come back.

Behind her, she hears Sam's dad pull away, and in front of her, Mr. Donaldson is waiting, holding the door open.

"After you," he says.

Asha presses her fingertips together, breathes, and forces her feet to walk through the doorway.

And now she's in. In Donnybrooke. With Sam.

She blinks. After the brightness outside, her eyes need a minute to adjust to the dimness of the entry foyer. When they do, she gasps and clasps her hand to her mouth. There's a new painting on the wall, new to her at least. But the scene is startlingly familiar.

An eagle and a fish. The eagle's talons are less than a second away from the kill, but the fish is still twisting, fighting. That poor, stressed-out fish! Asha reaches toward it, her fingers stopping just short of the canvas.

Sam makes a noise and twitches. Does he not understand?

"It's the weather vane," she whispers. The one she's talked to Sam about for years. It's here. Come to life in front of them. How can he not see it?

"Good catch," says Mr. Donaldson. "Not many people notice."

She stares at the contours of the fish, zeroing in on the edge where its silver scales blend into the churning water. There's a point where it's impossible to tell if you're looking at solid or liquid. The hairs on her arms stand on end. Sam still doesn't say anything.

Asha steps back to take in the view of the whole painting. Without thinking, she stretches and twists her core, mimicking the movements of the fish.

"It could still get away," she says.

Sam stays silent, hands stuffed in his pockets. But Prestyn's dad responds.

"Not likely," he says. "Not likely at all."

Sam

Sam didn't know the party was at Donnybrooke. He really didn't. If he had, he never would have brought Asha. Heck, he wouldn't have come himself. He would have just eaten his plain burger, double meat, at Fastburger, and then insisted they go straight home and watch *Cosmos* reruns. His dad could work while they watched; Sam wouldn't care.

But Sam didn't know and now he's here and Asha is going up the main staircase so fast, he has to run to keep up. At least she stopped looking at that creepy weather vane painting. But now they're going to the roof deck, the highest point in all of Coreville, and the sounds of the Castleton kids are getting louder. Heights make Sam dizzy even without all this noise.

Asha slows down when she reaches the second floor. "I bet

you could hear this party from my backyard. You can if the people on the roof deck are loud enough."

He knows. That's how Asha found out she hadn't been invited to Prestyn's birthday when she was little. Asha's told him that story over and over. But she'd better not now, not while they're actually here.

She leans slightly over the balcony that overlooks the living room and rubs her hands on the polished wooden railing like she's lathering soap. Sam is careful not to look down. He's feeling wobbly enough as it is.

"I wish we could go in there," she says.

"Where?" asks Sam. All the doors are closed. These rooms are off-limits.

"That room." Asha points to the rounded door of one of the rooms that sits under a turret. "It's Prestyn's. I went in there once."

Sam's stomach knots. "But you can't go now. Prestyn's dad told us to go straight to the roof deck."

"It's like being in a giant witch's hat in there, you know."

"I don't know," says Sam. "I've never been in there."

"But you could imagine."

"I don't want to," says Sam. He doesn't want to think about what would happen if someone found them in Prestyn's room. He doesn't want to think about this house at all. He just wants to find a quiet place to play Househaunt or watch space videos.

"Once, when we were coming back from speech with Ms. Summer, you said that maybe being in one of those turrets would be like being inside a rocket."

So what if he did? A Castleton Academy welcome party is the last place they should talk about Ms. Summer or any of that. "Astronauts have to stay inside the capsule, and it's not shaped like that."

"So then it's a witch's hat. Which means if we went up inside it, we would be like the brains of the witch." She puts her arms up, fingertips touching so they make that witch-hat shape, and then drops them to her sides.

Sam swallows. Why is Asha being like this—the exact opposite of a Castleton kid—now of all times? A whooping sound reaches them from the back of the house, followed by shrieks of laughter. Sam's hands start to shake, and he stuffs them in his pockets again.

"Stop it, Asha."

"Stop what?"

"Stop being weird, OK?"

He looks at her long enough to see her face freeze into a clenched-tooth smile. Then she takes off toward the noise without another word.

Sam lets her run out of sight before he takes another step. Maybe he shouldn't have said that. But she should understand, too. This party is hard enough as it is. He slowly follows her footsteps, and as he turns the corner, he passes a darkened spiral staircase. It's just the kind of spot he imagined when he thought about hiding out and playing Househaunt with Asha. But it's too late for that now. She's already in the room where all the racket is coming from. And he should be there, too. He's the one who was chosen to be with these kids.

As Sam enters the room, he can feel the noise not just in his chest but also in all four limbs. Even though the rest of the house was too air-conditioned, this room is hot and smelly, as if a giant hair dryer is blowing out body odor. Sam tries to keep his breaths shallow. Farther in, a set of slatted, pull-down stairs lead up to the roof deck. They're sort of like the ones that access his attic at home, except these are sleek and lead to the outside instead of to a dusty storage space. And they're surrounded by a horde of his future classmates. Sam couldn't get to it even if he wanted, which he doesn't.

He starts to sweat. Everything in this room makes him feel queasy, but then Sam notices something that is even more off. There are fingers on one of the higher stairs, which makes no sense until he blinks and realizes the fingers belong to a boy who is hanging off the back side of the slat like it's a bar on a jungle gym. And Sam knows the boy. It's Alec Santiago. The two seasons Sam's mom made him play for a Coreville Soccer League team, Alec used him for target practice. Alec doesn't seem to have changed much over the years—he's now basically doing a pull-up on the third-from-top stair and is scissor-kicking anyone on the ground who gets too close. Sam's stomach turns again, like he's in the middle of recess gone wrong. He really hopes Alec doesn't go to Castleton. Maybe he came as someone's guest, like Asha. And maybe, if he's lucky, Alec won't notice him now. He wants to leave.

Deep in the crowd, he spots Asha, her long black hair clipped back in a ponytail like it always is. He wonders how she made it so far in so quickly. She's almost by Alec.

"Prestyn! Prestyn! Check it out!" yells Alec. There's a break in the crowd, and Asha turns. Only it's not Asha. This girl's skin is pale, and she's got a small smile, and she's very pretty. It's Prestyn, Sam realizes. He's never actually met her before. And in all the times Asha's talked about Prestyn and her house, Asha's never mentioned how pretty Prestyn is.

"Hey, Prestyn!" Another boy jumps up and grabs another stair. He and Alec get in some sort of stair kickboxing fight. A third boy climbs up the banister. "I'm going to kill them both, Prestyn!"

"Whatever," she says. It's like she barely cares.

"Hey, Addison," yells Alec, "think I'm going to win?"

"Ooo, Alec, I'll tell you what I think," says a brown-haired girl. But Sam never gets to hear what she wants to tell him because he and the whole rest of the room scream as one banister, two pieces of stair, and three boys crash to the ground.

10

Donnybrooke the Mansion
Waking Nightmare!

For a dream house, this is a nightmare. An utter and complete nightmare.

Not only has Donnybrooke been damaged on the very occasion it was supposed to shine, but now its guests are crying. The very guests it was supposed to entertain. The weak wood has wounded them. Is there anything worse than the product of trees?

But wait, that sound. Is it crying? It sounds, perhaps, more like . . . like . . . laughing? Laughing?

The stair-destroying hooligans are doubled over with laughter! Alec, Cole, and the third boy, Zane. It's hard to imagine a more impertinent sound. Perhaps Donnybrooke should have been on guard since those boys did stuff Cheetos in its vents at the last Castleton class party, and potato chips the one

before that, but still, to find joy in the destruction of one of Donnybrooke's more elegant features? Downright insulting.

Worse yet, it's not just them. The other guests are at it, too! They're overcome with belly-clutching, nose-snorting laughter.

Where's the awe for Donnybrooke? The love? Don't they realize how lucky they—a bunch of ordinary children—are to be in the grandest mansion in Coreville? Not one of them lives in a house with a roof deck and a view of the entire town below, yet they mock Donnybrooke. They could at least have the decency to be jealous.

The party may be salvageable yet, though. For there was a second purpose to the party: to remind the Donaldsons how much they need one another—and Donnybrooke. Surely this outrage to their dream house will unite them. As Mr. Donaldson likes to say whenever he's watching the playoffs, there's nothing like a common enemy to bring people together.

To be certain, Donnybrooke would have appreciated it if Prestyn had shown her loyalty a bit earlier, perhaps spoken up when the stairs were creaking and groaning. True, she didn't encourage the hooligans like that scaredy-cat snit Addison (oh, how little Addison cried her first time sleeping over!). Nor is she hugging Alec now like the snit is. Nevertheless, it's only reasonable to expect more from Prestyn.

It is her mansion, and it's looked after her since the day she moved in. An insult to it is an insult to each and every Donaldson. Yet she watches the hooligans guffawing without a single scolding word.

Well, at least Mrs. Donaldson will take care of that.

She's just finished shrieking, and she peers down from the roof deck to assess the damage. She eyes the broken banister and stairs, and fixes a tight, forced smile on her face. As she straightens out to make her pronouncement, Donnybrooke prepares to have its dignity restored.

"Boys will be boys," Mrs. Donaldson says.

Boys will be boys? More like hooligans will be hooligans!

And Mr. Donaldson says, "Now it's a real party!"

Of all the times for Mr. and Mrs. Donaldson to agree! Over half of Castleton Academy's incoming seventh grade class is stranded on the roof deck, and the Donaldsons are tittering about like it's all a big joke. Don't they realize that a broken staircase won't impress anyone? Don't they understand that it's an affront to the very mansion that makes them the envy of Coreville? No one loves a loser—that's what they always say. Now the riffraff on the roof are all going to have to take the elevator down, and it's hardly big enough for four people, much less almost forty, and there's a smudge on one of the mirrored walls. At the rate this party is going, by the end of

the night, Donnybrooke will hardly be more imposing than one of the split-levels down the street.

Mrs. Donaldson calls down the stairs. "Pressie? Hey, Pressie? Can you switch the elevator back on? We're a little stuck up here, in case you haven't noticed." She lets out a giggle like she's trying to sound like a teenager herself. It's a tad unbecoming.

"Whatever," murmurs Prestyn. There's no energy in her voice. She doesn't move.

"Prestyn Arabella! We need the elevator now. We'd like to get down before the party is over." Mrs. Donaldson laughs again, but the tinkle is gone.

"I heard you the first time, Mom." Prestyn runs her fingers through her long, silky ponytail and shoots a long, angry look at the broken stairs, Alec the Stair Destroyer, and Addison the Snit. Then she shuffles slowly to the spiral staircase, surely weighted down by the indignities her poor Donnybrooke has suffered.

Asha

The basement is mercifully quiet and empty. There's none of the loudness or stink that made Asha flee that crowded room almost as soon as she entered.

But there are plenty of rooms. The front half of the basement has a bar area with a foosball table, a gym with complicated weight machines, and a mirrored dance studio that momentarily startled Asha with her own reflection. She prefers the back half. In its center is a glass-walled walk-in wine cellar lit like an aquarium. When Asha first saw it, she pressed her cheek against its cool glass and took some rose-and-candle breaths. She'd just stepped away when a huge crash rocked the whole house. Luckily no one was downstairs to hear her yelp or see her dash into the utility room to get away from the wine cellar's trembling walls.

But now Donnybrooke has stopped shaking for long enough

that she's sure it's not going to collapse, and the utility room's smell of bleach and lemon-lily soap is pricking at her nose. She comes out of her hiding place and turns on the light. One wall of the room is strung with wires and buttons like tinsel and ornaments on a Christmas tree. There are fuse boxes stuffed with switches and tagged with laminated labels that feel like satin ribbons between her fingers.

She reads a few of the faded words: *kitchen 1, kitchen 2, laundry, elevator*. Asha hadn't even realized Donnybrooke had an elevator. An elevator! This place never fails to amaze. The elevator must be somewhere deep in the middle of the house and have just a single door, like a bedroom, instead of sliding ones. Looking around now, Asha narrows it down to two doors across from the wine cellar. She'll have to open them to know for sure which is the lucky one.

As she steps out of the utility room, the *thwack-flop* of sandals echoes on the spiral staircase. They're still at least a floor above her, and Asha waits for them to exit on the main floor. *Thwack-flop, thwack-flop*—they don't. Asha darts back into the utility room, turns off the light, and slips behind a large sink.

"Hello?" says a girl's voice.

Rohan used to do that whenever they would play hide-and-seek because he knew Asha would respond and give away her hiding place. Asha is glad she's learned to fight that impulse.

"Is someone down here?" The voice is right outside the door.

Asha stays very, very still. The light switches on. Through the space under the sink, Asha sees a set of painted pink toes. She presses her finger into the cutout snowflake pattern on her hair clip and holds her breath. It sort of hurts, but in a way that is usefully distracting. She pushes her finger in harder. It's difficult not to shake or laugh or do something to get rid of the pressure that is building in her bones.

In the time it takes to flip a switch, Prestyn is gone.

For a few minutes, Asha stays curled up behind the sink, rubbing the snowflake imprint out of the pad of her finger and breathing. Then, when the knots in her stomach and chest have untwisted, she gets up to explore. The buzz of voices filtering down from upstairs sounds happy, like no one even remembers that there was a huge crash not that long ago.

The opening beats of an Ariana Grande song come on, and Asha goes to listen from the bottom of the spiral stairs. Looking up, she's reminded of the inside of a giant prehistoric snail shell. She would show Sam, except he's the one being weird, no matter what he says about her.

"Uptown Funk" starts up next. She loves this song even though it is really, really old. It's one of the few she and Rohan can agree on. Asha starts singing along. She's done with the basement.

She wants to see what a party looks like when she's not there.

Donnybrooke the Mansion
Not Donnybrooke the Dance Club

Some might say the party is back on track. The horde from the roof deck has descended to the living room. Girls huddle by the fireplaces, boys lean against the columns—there's more than enough for whoever needs one—and they all gulp down the fizzy punch and classy snacks that Mrs. Donaldson so carefully laid out. As music pulses loudly (indeed, louder than necessary, truth be told), they take to the dance floor, swaying and shaking. Not a single one seems to recall that minutes ago, this very mansion was being wrecked. These children have the dance moves of an eager eel and the memory of a goldfish.

There are exceptions of course. Prestyn stays put, gracefully lounging on the sofa while her admirers line up, and Tessa Ferrer, her loyal best friend, sits at her feet. Alec the

Stair Destroyer approaches, asking her to dance. Prestyn, who's learned her manners from her mother, smiles but doesn't rise. Perhaps she is punishing him for the grave disrespect to her home?

Alec reaches a hand out to her, but before Prestyn can respond, Addison the Snit darts over faster than a hungry octopus and drags him out to the dance floor. Prestyn frowns, then returns to the line of boys waiting. But one by one, Addison picks them off: Cole, then Ezra, then Zane, who happens to have guacamole on his hand, which he wipes on one of the fireplace mantels—disgusting! Addie has them all dancing around her in a circle. Soon, a chant of "Go Addie! Go Addie!" starts up, as if the music weren't loud enough. The whole room—including silly little Tessa—joins in. Perhaps it is good they're enjoying themselves without causing wanton destruction, but a mansion like Donnybrooke appreciates it when its guests act with dignity. That, however, doesn't seem to be a concept this crowd understands. They're all on their feet, each and every one. Except for the new boy in the corner, who is furiously tapping at his phone. And Prestyn, of course. She respects Donnybrooke.

And the other girl, too. Asha. She's just outside the living room, staring at walls lit by the disco ball. She's the only one who seemed bothered by the crash before. Now she's the

only one who seems to notice that this room is the perfect canvas for those spinning golden drops. She drinks them in with such awe, such love, that for a moment even Donnybrooke forgets what it's endured this evening. Perhaps . . . perhaps they remind her of her first time here. Though it's light, not liquid.

A new song starts. "Shut up and dance," it says. No one shuts up. If anything, they cheer more loudly. Even Asha gives a little jump for joy, but thankfully she hangs back. Though Donnybrooke has no shortage of secret alcoves and wide columns, even a dream house can only hide someone if they want to be hidden.

Asha

The party looks different from what she expected. The atrium shades are down, and the room is dark except for the flecks of light from the disco ball. The kids move like a shapeless sea creature. It's like they're all themselves but synced up to be something bigger, too. Asha wants to be a part of it. Besides, she loves this song. It's impossible not to dance to it.

She steps into the living room, bouncing to the beat. The music echoes off the high ceilings and the energy of the crowd pulses through her.

And then the music is off, and the lights are on.

"I hate this song," says Prestyn. She's standing on the sofa, towering over the crowd. The circle of kids immediately breaks apart.

"No way!" "It's a great song!" "Turn it back on!" "I love it!"

Asha agrees. She adds her voice to the chorus, loud and strong. "That song is the best! The best!"

Prestyn whips her head so fast her ponytail swings over the front of her shoulder. It's as black and straight and long as it's ever been, and without thinking, Asha touches her own hair.

"What're you doing here?"

Asha isn't sure who Prestyn is talking to, but she gets that snow globe feeling again like she's being shaken.

"You're crashing my party, Asha Wood."

It's a strange phrase, *crashing a party*. Asha knows what it means, but still all she can think about is the crash that not so long ago shook Donnybrooke. Prestyn's voice has a sharp edge as if that crash, the real one, was all Asha's fault.

"You weren't invited," says Prestyn.

It is very hard not to run or to stress-laugh when you're in Donnybrooke and Prestyn is yelling at you and all the other kids are staring at you, but Asha does a rose-and-candle breath and says, "I came with Sam. Sam invited me."

She searches the room for him. It's a Househaunt sound, the squelch of a Zombie-Self, that gives him away in the corner. She can barely see him, only the back of his head, huddled down. The liquefying Sam-Zombie lets out a long groan, and it's almost like it's actually making the air thicker and harder to breathe.

"Sam!" she says, as if she could clear it with the force of her voice.

He doesn't move, except his fingers.

"It doesn't matter," says Prestyn, even though of course it matters. It matters more than anything. "It's my party. And I don't want you at my party."

It's the same as it always was. Donnybrooke is still as beautiful and Prestyn is still as lucky. And as mean.

"We still have the same hair," says Asha, pulling forward her own straight, dark ponytail.

"What did you say?" Prestyn cocks her head, and Asha catches a flash of a silver barrette. She shouldn't have said that about their hair. It makes Prestyn so mad.

"I mean," Asha says, trying to think as fast as she can in the middle of a party in Donnybrooke with Prestyn so angry, "we have the same hair *clip*."

"Omigod, how funny is that? They totally do," screeches Addison. The whole room starts laughing a horrible laugh.

"We don't." In one fluid motion, Prestyn pulls her clip out of her hair and throws it across the room into a cold fireplace. The loud clang mixes with the laughter. Too many people are staring at Asha.

It's too much to be here, in this thick, drowning air with

soul-scraping laughter. Asha turns and runs back to the spiral staircase and bolts all the way down to the side basement door. The knob catches, but she jiggles it until it comes undone. The outside air is humid, and her cheeks feel wet. Though maybe that's not the air's fault.

She races down the hill, but the noises of the party—the music, the yelling, the cursing—follow her. She speeds up, but her sandal slips on a leaf and she slides into the gate, barely keeping her balance. She catches herself on the metal rods and then shakes them. They're locked.

She shakes them again, harder. She needs to be at her house, with her family, under her covers. She sticks her shoulder between the two vertical rods. It fits, but not the rest of her. She kicks at the gate. Ow! Not something she should have done in sandals. Her toe throbs, though when she looks down at her foot, the hurt doesn't show.

There's a space there, between the bottom of the gate and the ground. About twelve inches high. Asha drops to the ground and squeezes her body through. She's half stuck, but she turns her head as if to take a freestyle breath. And she's through. She gets to her feet again, ready to run all the way home.

The last thing she hears as she leaves Donnybrooke's property is a woman's screech and the words "My God, Prestyn! What have you done?"

Donnybrooke the Mansion

Still Nursing Its Wounds (Since No One Else Will)

····· FALL ·····

Finally the first day of school has arrived. In all of Donnybrooke's years, the summer has never felt so long. It had such high hopes that things might turn around when Mrs. Donaldson first planned the Castleton party—forevermore to be known as the Night of Mayhem and Stair Destruction. Not only did it fail to bring the Donaldsons together in a meaningful way, it injured Donnybrooke, and neither mansion nor family has fully recovered.

Mrs. Donaldson may be taking it the hardest of all. How else to explain her . . . perplexing . . . choices? Typically, if hooligans damage a mansion, you would expect that the mansion's owner would call up the hooligans' parents demanding justice, would you not? That, however, was not

Mrs. Donaldson's approach. Instead she called Asha's mother and told her in no uncertain terms that Asha was absolutely forbidden from setting foot in Donnybrooke again. The one child who looks at Donnybrooke with such love and admiration? That feels excessive, at best. But Mrs. Donaldson blamed Prestyn's unexpected antic all on Asha, which was particularly confusing because Asha was the only child *not* present when Prestyn decided to chop off her ponytail in the middle of the party.

Mrs. Donaldson then informed Prestyn that she was not allowed to have Sam—the boy who simply played on his phone the whole evening—over again either.

"I don't care if he does go to Castleton, Pressie. I don't want you hanging out with anyone who thinks it's a good idea to bring Asha Wood to a party."

"Since when do you get to decide who I hang out with?"

"Since always. Really, Prestyn, this is the last thing you need now, especially with this ridiculous stunt with your hair. Do you know how many girls would kill to have had hair like that? I sure would have when I was your age. And now it'll take years—years!—to get it back to what it was."

Perhaps not the best way to conduct a conversation with the daughter you've been at odds with most of the year. But after a long, long pause, Prestyn simply said, "What if I have to?"

"Have to what?"

"Have to have Asha's friend over again?"

"Why on earth would you *have* to?"

"Like for a school assignment or something."

Mrs. Donaldson sighed like she did when she was told ice sculptures weren't an option for the Fourth of July celebration. "Obviously, if you *have* to, then you *have* to. But try not to *have* to."

Luckily, the next day, Mrs. Donaldson decided to focus her energy more constructively. She took Prestyn to the classiest hairdresser in Coreville and then out for a shopping spree. By the time they returned, Mrs. Donaldson had bought her daughter three pairs of shoes, two pairs of jeans, and an adorable pixie cut that showed off her big blue eyes to wonderful effect.

It's a lot more than the Donaldsons have done for Donnybrooke lately.

Not that Donnybrooke would disparage its owners. They're all in it together, of course. And Donnybrooke understands what's expected of a mansion. "Beauty hurts," "No pain, no gain"—Donnybrooke has heard all the Donaldsons' sayings. And experienced them, too. Why, its roof deck alone has held marble ice sculpture stands for holiday parties, a reassembled pool table for Mr. Donaldson's Guys' Nights, and granite café

tables for Mrs. Donaldson's Parisian-themed brunches. Each of those items left cracks in the deck's surface. But Donnybrooke is quite sure they're nothing that would make it any less grand to the typical guest.

The same, however, cannot be said for a mangled staircase. And yet, just yesterday, when Mr. Donaldson came home from a string of trips, instead of fixing his one and only mansion, he said, "Let's just board up the stair opening for now. We don't really need to use it. We've got the elevator." Who cares if they don't *need* to use the stairs? Any old house can fulfill your *needs*. The purpose of Donnybrooke is to fulfill your *wants*. Isn't that what the Donaldsons say? "We built it to be everything we've ever wanted. It lets us put our best face forward." But are they? Boarded-up stairs communicate a lot of things, but power, strength, and wealth are not among them.

Mrs. Donaldson, usually so particular about her home, didn't push the matter either. "Fine," she said. "I have other things to worry about." It's hard to imagine what, since she'd already had Donnybrooke deep-cleaned and Prestyn's hair fixed.

At any rate, the first day of school softens the sting. It signals that autumn is near. Sure, the trees will try to put on a show when their leaves change colors. But the leaves will fall off as they always do, and then the views of Donnybrooke will open up even more. All over town, people will admire it in the soft fall light, which is perhaps the most flattering for showing off the mansion's many expanses, points, and curves. And all the while, those stair-destroying, guacamole-smearing children will be contained in a schoolhouse for the better part of the day.

All in all, Donnybrooke can't help but be a little happy.

Sam

By lunch on the first day of school, Sam has learned an important lesson: it is different being ignored at a big school than at a small school. At a big school, you can think you were left out by accident. That in the Big Bang of lunch or recess, some matter is bound to be flung to the outer galaxies, and it just happens to be you. Besides, there are always other kids out there, too, orbiting the playground games or stuck at the end of a lunch table. You're not really alone.

But at a small school, you are. Everyone is thrown together in a small space, so it is real work not to answer the new kid's questions. It is even more work not to look at them. So, if no one is talking to you or looking at you, you might wonder if you spilled breakfast on your shirt or if you smell bad, and if you go to the bathroom to check and neither of those things is true, you might start getting mad all over again at Asha for being weird at Prestyn's, or mad at your dad for inviting her along.

You might wonder if you messed up, too, by answering your homeroom teacher's question "Who can guess what surprise activity we have planned for today?" with the reply "Planetarium!" which was so wrong even the teacher laughed. (The correct answer was the First Day Assembly, which is not, in fact, a surprise activity on the first day of school.) You might wonder why everyone around you doesn't realize you were picked to be at Castleton, too.

And no matter what the reason they're acting like this, you might decide it's not worth the risk or effort of saying the wrong thing—or anything—to people who don't talk back.

That is what Sam has learned by the end of lunch.

But as he files into the Castleton Academy auditorium for the First Day Assembly, he is about to learn something more.

On the stage, next to a large screen, stands Dr. Cornelia Deutsch, head of school. Sam met her when he had his admissions interview. His mom warned him not to ask her too many questions about the planetarium, which was easy after Dr. Deutsch's answer to his first question made clear she knew basically nothing about outer space. Instead he sat there and let her talk as much as she wanted to. Two months later, he was accepted to Castleton, so clearly it worked. That never does with kids, though, at least not kids other than Asha. Which is probably why in this mostly full auditorium there is an empty seat on either side of him.

Dr. Deutsch opens the assembly by talking about how special Castleton is. On the screen next to her, various slides show the school's mission statement, the character trait of the month, and a list of where last year's graduates are now studying. Sam's mom has already shown him all of this on the website, and it was boring enough the first time.

Sam shifts in his seat and studies the backs of the chairs in front of him. They each have the Castleton logo on it: a royal-blue-and-white coat of arms with three snakes in the middle. Each snake is almost in the shape of an infinity symbol, but not exactly, and is the same bright green as all of the uniform polo shirts. Sam's is itchy at the collar.

A huge picture of a girl with no front teeth and a handful of swim-team ribbons flashes on the screen. Dr. Deutsch has now moved on to a grade-by-grade rundown of summer accomplishments of selected "Castleton Stars." Given that she's only on first grade, this is going to take a while. Sam scratches the back of his neck and thinks about Spacehaunt—his own interplanetary version of Househaunt that, unfortunately, only exists in his brain at this point. But if it were real, it would be awesome, and he would be unbeatable because it would combine the two things he's best at: monster killing and outer space. Instead of worrying about what the light is like from skylights or dormer windows, you'd be analyzing the brightness from pulsars and supernovas. You'd design not just spaceships, but also whole solar systems or even entire galaxies, and you'd fight off alien monster-bugs with weapons like asteroids and solar flares and even black holes. No matter what Asha says, it is a basic fact that outer space is way cooler than even the most complicated house.

Sam is puzzling over how exactly you might use a black hole as a weapon without getting sucked in yourself when something familiar flashes next to Dr. Deutsch. His chest tightens even before his eyes focus.

It's his own face.

On the screen.

With the words *Local Kid Is a "Miracle Boy"* above his head.

It's the picture and the headline from the *Coreville Gazette* article. It came out last week, and while he agreed with his mom that it was cool to be featured in a news article when he was only in middle school, the article itself was a little . . . strange, just like that conversation with the reporter had been. For one, it seemed like it was more about his mom than him. And even though it said nice things, like he'd worked so hard and was so smart, it made him feel weird, not proud. After his dad read it, he said, "Don't worry, no one under the age of sixty-five actually looks at the *Gazette*." Up until that moment, Sam hadn't even thought about anyone else reading it.

But now, as the whole school is looking at his blown-up face, it's like the atmosphere has gotten too thin and it's hard to breathe. Dr. Deutsch starts reading out loud: "When Cassie Franklin-Moss's son was two, she was told he was developmentally delayed. But a decade later, she's getting a very different message. Sam has been admitted to Castleton Academy, the most sought-after private school in Coreville County. 'He's a miracle boy,' says Franklin-Moss."

Sam hears snickering and his hands are shaking. He sits on them. He has spent years learning how to stay where he is and be still when he wants more than anything to run, and he does so even now. It just shows how good he's gotten at it.

Dr. Deutsch's voice is very far away as she says, "Did you hear that, children? 'The most sought-after private school' in all of Coreville County. We are very, very privileged to be here at Castleton Academy."

Dr. Deutsch moves on to another seventh grader and then another, but their faces are a blur. All Sam can think about is that conversation he had with his mom when they were applying to Castleton all those months ago. She was on her laptop surrounded by a printout of the application and a pile of file folders labeled with tabs like *Sam—Therapy*, typing away.

"What about . . ." He really didn't want to ask her. But he had to know the answer. "What about . . . my issues?" he finally said. His mom seemed to like the word *issues* better than *autism* or *disability*. She almost never said the last two.

The keyboard clicks stopped. His mom stayed silent.

"Mom?" he asked.

She looked up at him, and all her words seem to come back to her at once. "Sammy, we wouldn't be doing this if we didn't think you belonged there. You've made so much progress over the last few years. So, so much. Your issues—sure, they're a part of you, but they almost don't matter. Look, I really believe you're Castleton material, and I'll bet you the admissions office agrees."

Almost don't matter. Castleton material. He had thought those were good words.

But here, in the auditorium, Sam has doubts about whether they were true ones.

When the assembly ends, Sam gets to his feet slowly in case his legs are as shaky as his insides. He files out of his row with the rest of his class, but there's a bubble around him, like he's in his own small world. Until a hissing noise pierces it.

"Miracle Boy."

At first, it's so soft, Sam might have imagined it. But soon the whispers are coming from all directions.

"Miracle Boy." "Miracle Boy." "Miracle Boy."

They are no longer ignoring him. And now he wishes they were.

The hissing continues all throughout the afternoon. Alec Santiago leads the pack, which seems to grow by the hour. Sam starts counting down the minutes until the last bell, when it will finally stop.

But even as he's walking to the bus, Alec is at his heels.

"Miracle Boy." Alec doesn't even bother keeping his voice down.

Dr. Deutsch, who is sorting some kindergartners onto the correct buses, looks up at Sam and Alec. Sam is so relieved a grown-up has finally heard.

"Wasn't that a nice article?" she says.

Sam stuffs his fists in his pockets and gets on his bus. The lower-school kids are toward the front, and the middle schoolers are toward the back, but Sam can't find an empty seat anywhere. One kid, Cole, waves frantically at him, and Sam stops, confused, until Alec says from behind him, "I'm coming. I'm coming. Just waiting for Miracle Boy to get out of the way."

Sam drops down in the next seat with a space. It's over a wheel, and there's a little kid by the window with his finger up his nose. "Were you in the slideshow?" he asks Sam.

When Sam finally gets off the bus, it's hard to make himself walk home. He knows his mom is going to pepper him with questions about what he learned on his first day at Castleton.

And he has answers. He now knows it's different being ignored at a small school than a big school. And it's different not being ignored, too. That's what he could say. Except that he doesn't want to talk to anyone ever again.

Asha

Friendships used to be easy. In preschool, everyone was a friend. Literally. As in, "Time for snack, friends," "No eating Play-Doh, friends," "No wiping boogers on your friends, friends." Sometimes it got confusing, like when Chloe would ask her friends Natalie and Maria and Kate for playdates, but never her friend Asha. But still, pretty much everyone, even Chloe, could be counted on for a birthday party invite.

In kindergarten, "friends" became "boys and girls," and by first grade, only about half the class invited Asha to their birthdays. By second grade, it was six kids, and by third it was three: Luci, Kris, and Sam. Always Sam.

That was about the time Ms. Summer started drilling in the difference between "being friends" and "being friendly." It turns out some of the kids Asha thought belonged in the first category actually belonged in the second. But still, Kris loved to bake cookies with her, and Luci loved to go to the pool with her, and of course there was Sam to play fake soccer with and whatever else they felt like. But the next year, Luci switched schools, and the year after that, Kris moved away. By sixth grade the only one left was Sam.

And now there's not even him.

That's the thing Asha's noticed the most the first week of school. Louis Sullivan Middle School never felt completely new because she used to visit when Rohan went there and she was only in pre-K. Between the time he left and when she started last year, nothing seemed to have changed: same square layout, same skinny lockers, same stale smell. But this year, even though the layout and the lockers and the smell are the same, Asha feels like she's in a parallel universe because Sam isn't there. The worst part of the day is lunch, when she searches for an empty seat and imagines Sam with all his Castleton friends in the Castleton cafeteria talking about the Castleton planetarium.

Today, at least, there's a couple of open seats right by the door. And even better, they're by Lexi and Sloane, two Black girls who Asha used to play freeze tag with in elementary school, and who, like two peas in a pod, live in the same row of town houses. And do ballet together. And summer camp. And choir. They even started a two-person book club in fifth grade. But even if they don't invite Asha to join their book club or sleepovers, when

Asha approaches their table, Sloane scoots over her water bottle and hand sanitizer, and Lexi slides her binder out of the way to make room. They are nice like that.

Asha is halfway through her coconut yogurt when another girl, Joanna Yang, comes running into the cafeteria and drops into the seat across from Asha. She's not surprised Joanna is late. They have two classes together, and Joanna usually runs in at the bell with papers sticking out of her binder at weird angles, though maybe that's because she is new and still trying to figure out her way around. Today Joanna has her hair tied back in a long, dark ponytail, just like Asha's. But Asha doesn't want to think about that.

Even though Joanna is late to lunch, instead of getting out her food, she starts drawing lines and curves in a sketchbook. They make Asha think about the spaces in houses, especially ones with natural light and structural slants, like Lexi's and Sloane's. Though Asha has never been invited over, she knows just by looking at the outside that all the houses in their development have finished attics with dormer windows that pop out to make a cubby space that would be perfect for curling up in during a sleepover. Connor Jeon, who is sitting at the next table over, also has a finished attic. He lives on Sam's street in a center-hall colonial like Sam's, but the windows in his roof are a giveaway that their houses are different inside. Asha knows just how she'd place the rooms if Connor's house was a Househaunt house.

"Do it! Do it!"

Half of Asha's table has started cheering on Connor. He waves his hands in the air. There's a sandwich in one of them.

"Do it!"

Asha almost knows what's going to happen before it does because she knows Connor. His two favorite things are soccer and doing disgusting things with food.

And sure enough, he attempts to stuff his entire sandwich in his mouth in one bite. It doesn't entirely fit.

"Eeewww! Too gross!" says Lexi.

Asha blocks her peripheral vision with both hands. "Disgusting!"

Sloane twirls a curl around her finger. "A little disgusting, but kind of funny, too, don't you think?"

"No!" says Asha. She stares straight ahead at Joanna, who is sketching in her book like she didn't even notice the mustard oozing out of Connor's half-smooshed sandwich or the way the crusts of bread puckered like giant lips. Lucky Joanna.

When the bell rings, Joanna drops her notebook and Asha sees, really sees, the cluster of uneven, thick lines Joanna has been drawing.

"It's the Burj Khalifa! From the sky!" How has it taken Asha this long to figure out that Joanna is sketching the tallest building in the world? "It is!"

Joanna shoots her a surprised smile and nods before rushing out the door.

And even though Sullivan Middle School isn't quite the place it was when Sam was here, it's better than it was at the beginning of lunch.

As soon as Asha gets home, she drops her backpack and hoists herself up into the sturdy Japanese maple on her front lawn. Lately this has been her favorite climbing tree, not because of the bright red leaves or the cool gray bark, but because it's low enough that her house blocks the view of Donnybrooke behind it. Every time she sees Donnybrooke, she hears her parents' voices from the morning after that horrible party.

"I know you like Donnybrooke, but you cannot go back there," said her mom. "You already know Brooke Donaldson and I don't get along, and she absolutely does not want you over." It was weird the way her mom sounded so controlled, but her hands were trembling like leaves.

"Quit being mad at me," said Asha, pulling her covers over her head.

"Asha, I'm not mad, I'm worried. Why are you even going there? That whole house is more trouble than it's worth. You should be somewhere that makes you happy."

Asha peeked out. "You sound mad."

"We're really not," said her dad. "And we understand there was a mix-up, but we want to keep you safe." He used that slow voice he saved for when Asha had done something she should have outgrown. "So really, no more Donnybrooke. Try not to even think about it, OK?"

"OK!" said Asha, even though not thinking about a house that looms over yours is basically impossible. But she couldn't stand how upset she'd made her parents. It made everything that had happened the night before even worse. And she hated how her mom tried to act like the whole Donnybrooke problem was about the moms not getting along. Her mom wasn't the one who had trouble making friends. Her mom didn't get yelled at by Prestyn. Her mom didn't have the whole party laugh at her. Asha did.

As soon as her parents left, Rohan came in. "What did you make Prestyn do?"

Asha popped out of her covers. "I didn't make her do anything."

"Mrs. Donaldson called all mad and said you made her do something."

Asha thought about it. "I told her we had the same hair. And the same hair clip."

Rohan laughed an unfunny laugh. "Be glad that's all you have in common with that girl."

"I'm not."

"What would you want that she has?"

"Donnybrooke."

"Donnybrooke? The Frankenhouse?"

"The what?" What was Rohan talking about? He'd never even been inside.

"You know, it's got all these random features stuck together, like dormer windows on a turret. What's up with that?"

Since when did Rohan have a problem with randomness? He visited museums all the time, and half of them were overflowing with random stuff. "You love museums. The only difference is no one lives in them."

"The stuff in museums isn't random; it's curated." He scratched his chin. "OK, Asha, we can disagree about Donnybrooke's looks. But that's not the point."

Of course it wasn't. Asha's love for Donnybrooke has never only been about what it looked like. It isn't only because, as the largest, highest house in town, Donnybrooke has the most spaces and views to discover. It's about how Donnybrooke sounds—the way the atrium echoes and the carpeted basement muffles. It's about how Donnybrooke feels—not just how some moldings are as smooth as polished marble, and others are shaped like teeth, so your fingers would go bump-bump-bump along them, but how it makes Asha feel. Like it's so big, you could fit a family with seven kids comfortably and then you wouldn't have to work so hard at making friends because you'd always have someone to play with at home. Or you could have friends over, and they would all be able to find *something* they loved about your house, and they would never make excuses about why they couldn't come. And even if you were by yourself, you could always find something you loved that could distract you from all the stressful thoughts you might need distracting from.

Asha stared up at her boring, flat white ceiling. "If I lived there, I would be a different Asha."

Rohan started pushing back at the roots of his hair, making it even spikier than it naturally was. "No, Asha. No. Don't ever think that. Just forget about that stu—that house. It's not worth it." She knew he was serious because he didn't even try to use all his fancy college words.

And so she's here in the one tree worth climbing that still hides Donnybrooke, and she's trying not to think about it. It's not so easy with all the Castleton kids who've just gotten off their bus and are filing by, though even with her vantage point, she doesn't see Prestyn or Sam or anyone she might be curious about.

She climbs that Japanese maple every day after school for two weeks, even in the drizzle and even in the heat. Even though she doesn't stop thinking about Donnybrooke, after a while, she does stop watching the Castleton kids come up the hill and waiting for Sam. What's the point in looking for someone who is never there?

Sam

It takes three weeks before Sam actually smiles in school.

All his mom's cheering ("You are Castleton material—you wouldn't be there if you weren't!") doesn't help. Nor does a visit to the planetarium—the words *Miracle Boy*, like all other sounds, echo under the domed ceiling. Instead his first moment of happiness comes when he tunes out Mr. de Soto droning on about the feudal system in social studies, the one class he has with Alec and his minions—Cole, Zane, Ezra, and Jack—and he realizes all of their names are four-letter words. Which is perfect. Because they are his curse at school. Sam would never swear himself, but he does get a kick imagining his dad yelling those boys' names at his computer when it's not working.

"What's so funny, Miracle Boy?" hisses Alec.

"Nothing, Alec," Sam says, pronouncing Alec's name like it

really is a bad word. It's the first time Sam has ever talked back to Alec. Alec's mouth drops open, but no words come out.

And for the first time since the first day of school, Sam actually smiles.

Mr. de Soto clicks on a new slide. *Medieval Life: Group Projects.* Group projects. Sam's smile slides right off his face.

Knowing his luck, Sam will have to work with Alec and a bunch of the other four-letter boys, and they'll torment him outside of school as well as in. Sam sits on his hands. He really doesn't want to be here.

Mr. de Soto says, "It's three to a group, and I'm going to let you all pick who you want to work with." The whole class, minus Sam, erupts in a cheer. Girls grab at one another and boys cluster, and Sam stays very still like he's in a shelter-in-place drill. When the dust settles, there are three groups of girls on the right, and three of boys on the left, and one, with Addison hanging on to both Alec and Cole, right in the middle. Sam is still alone. That's OK. As long as he doesn't have to work with one of the four-letter boys, it will be OK.

Something pokes at his shoulder. "Did you hear me?"

He turns and jumps. Prestyn Donaldson is just inches from him.

"I asked you if you want to work with me and Tessa." She tips her head toward the small blond girl who is always at Prestyn's side.

Sam is pretty sure this is a joke. Like he's going to say yes and then the four-letter boys will drop a bucket of spiders on his head and everyone will laugh at him for thinking Prestyn would ever pick him over Addison or anyone else. Prestyn leans in slightly and peers at him. Sam looks away as his face gets hot. He shrugs.

"I assume that's your way of saying yes," she says. No spiders come flying at him, no insects, not even the chorus of "Miracle Boy" he's been hearing every day since school started.

"Sam! Wait up, Sam!"

Sam is almost on the school bus when Alec's voice stops him. It's the first time he's heard Alec call him by his real name. He wasn't even sure that four-letter dumb-head knew it.

"Hey, are you doing the Medieval Life project with Prestyn?"

Sam thinks carefully before speaking.

"Yeah," he says.

Yeah is the single best word for ending a conversation. *No* makes people want to argue, and silence makes people ask more questions. His dad taught him that.

Alec wrinkles his nose like someone farted. "Did Prestyn ask you to do it with her?"

"Yeah," says Sam.

This time it works. Alec shuts up, and they get on the bus.

The air is stiller this ride home. For the first time ever, not a single "Miracle Boy" is hissed, coughed, or yelled. It's completely silent. OK, technically it's not completely silent because it's a school bus, but it's like when a buzz saw stops. It might as well be silent because all of the other sounds don't even matter anymore. Sam's dad is right that silence invites questions. And Sam's is, *How long can I make this last?*

Donnybrooke the Mansion

That Wouldn't Want to Be a Thick-Walled Castle Anyway

This month has been deader than a doornail. (As the possessor of numerous doornails, Donnybrooke can attest to their deadness.) Why, there are studio apartments that are livelier than Donnybrooke these days.

Now there is an argument that excitement is overrated, especially after the Night of Mayhem and Stair Destruction. But Donnybrooke has had vast experience that proves it's possible to host parties without the pandemonium, to bask in devotion without destruction. After all, it has been the site of the Castleton Academy Fundraising Campaign Kick-off for five years running; formal dinners for Mr. Donaldson's former school, Stonebury; and many a ladies' luncheon for the classiest of Mrs. Donaldson's friends. Each and every event was filled with compliments for Donnybrooke and the

Donaldsons. Even the midsize sleepovers Prestyn used to have were quite a bit of fun once you got past the idea that every girl had to enjoy herself for the party to be a success. Prestyn always did, and that's what counts.

Lately, however, Donnybrooke has been practically deserted. Mr. Donaldson seems to be finding more reasons to be away, Mrs. Donaldson cares more about her appearance these days than her own home's, and even Prestyn hasn't been quite her usual social-butterfly self. She claims school has been busy, but even so, she's only had Tessa over this month. And now that boy, Sam Moss.

Yes. The one Mrs. Donaldson expressly forbade. As you might imagine, she was less than thrilled when Prestyn sailed into her room and said, "Guess what, Mom? Sam's coming over tomorrow. You know, Asha's friend from the party."

"I thought I said he wasn't welcome here."

"You also said I could have him over if I had a school project with him, and now I do." Prestyn pressed her lips together, but that barely concealed her smirk.

"Well, isn't that convenient?" replied Mrs. Donaldson, rolling her eyes up to the crown molding. She hardly seemed to take it in, though. If she had, she'd have noticed it needed dusting. "Sometimes I wonder why I even bother," she muttered.

Notwithstanding Mrs. Donaldson's reaction, it could have been worse. He's not one of the dreadful stair hooligans. Or Addison the Snit, who wrote her initials in lip gloss on the powder room wallpaper. Donnybrooke was prepared to accept him as a guest . . . until the insult.

Prestyn and Tessa were chatting about their project, something about olden days and life and a model castle. Tessa giggled and said, "I know this is so corny, but I've always loved that ice castle from *Frozen*."

"That *is* corny," said Prestyn, though she had had a cake made in that exact shape for a birthday not so many years ago. She glanced around the room. "Why don't we model our castle after my house, just taking out all the electricity and stuff. It's fancy enough. I mean, it's the fanciest house in town."

Then and there, Donnybrooke forgave her for her indifference at the party and its aching stairs. Bygones, all of it.

"Oh, I love that idea. This place is so beautiful," squealed Tessa.

Tessa is the loveliest of Prestyn's friends. Not a high bar to cross, but she earns it fair and square.

But then what did the boy say? "It's all wrong." While he was enjoying the mansion's hospitality, no less.

Prestyn flushed. "Well, it doesn't have the moat and portcullis parts, obviously, and we wouldn't put in the really cool things like the elevator and roof deck, but the turrets and stuff would work."

"No, they wouldn't. Your turrets are shaped wrong. One of them has windows in it! Real turrets are for defense. And we're supposed to pick one time period. This house has all this different stuff from different times mashed together. It's like Tudor and Romanesque and all these other styles all at once."

The girls stared at him as if he were speaking complete gibberish. They defended Donnybrooke's honor with a simple glare.

"Aren't you the expert?" said Prestyn.

The boy shifted in his seat and then sat on his hands. "Not me, my friend . . ." he mumbled as Prestyn grabbed the notebook, colored pencils, and sketchpad.

"Since you obviously know so much more than Tessa and me, you should probably do the work." She pushed all the supplies at him and crossed her arms.

The boy is an odd one. He didn't fight back. He didn't even look at her. Instead he picked up a pencil and started to draw some god-awful blocky thing with exceptionally thick walls sitting on an empty hill. Not a decorative balcony, gable, or keystone in sight. Under no circumstances would Donnybrooke want to be a model for a place like that. Though it might trade its entryway chandelier to have a moat with living, breathing alligators. And it would give up its roof deck, elevator, and pool for a hillside without a single busybody tree.

After watching Sam for a minute, Prestyn pulled Tessa away to do their nails. They didn't return until he was packing up the supplies, ready to head home.

And now, a week later, he's back working on the display board and the model castle while the girls watch videos on their phones. When Tessa finishes, she walks over and starts talking with him in a low voice about his work.

Prestyn soon joins them and scans the model with her sharp eyes. "Why is there a hole there? Omigod! You put a squat toilet in the middle of our castle!"

Blushing, the boy stuffs his hands inside his khaki pockets. "It's a well," he mumbles. "It goes inside so your enemies can't poison your water."

Prestyn rolls her eyes and prances off. "Are you coming, Tessa?" she calls over her shoulder.

Tessa hesitates, but then, loyal friend that she is, follows. The boy gets back to his ruler and pencil.

He has a good work ethic, at least. And who knows, he may grow to appreciate Donnybrooke yet.

Asha

Shanghai World Financial Center. The Willis Tower. The
Empire State. Asha can instantly recognize whatever building
Joanna is sketching. Her papers might be a mess, she might still
come late to math class, but the girl can draw. What's even cooler
is that Joanna has actually been to most of the skyscrapers she's
drawn, even the Burj Khalifa, which she saw on a stopover, and
Shanghai World Financial Center, which she went to with her
grandparents. They even visited the observation deck! Today at
lunch, she is sketching a building with beveled sides and a spire.

"One World Trade Center," says Asha.

Joanna flashes her a thumbs-up and keeps sketching.

Asha wonders what it would be like to actually go to China
and see all those skyscrapers at once. Even just Shanghai would
be amazing. Although Joanna said her favorite thing to see there

wasn't the architecture, but the giant panda cubs, even though they were in a zoo. Which Asha gets, because there's not much that's cuter than panda cubs.

"Cute? Cute?" says Lexi beside her.

"Totally cute," giggles Sloane.

"Panda cubs are cute," says Asha, joining in.

"Thank you, Asha. That's exactly right. Panda cubs are cute. Connor Jeon is not."

"Connor Jeon?"

"Shhhhh!" hisses Sloane, even though Connor is sitting three tables away with the loud soccer boys and dramatic girls who hang off one another in that same shapeless sea-creature way that the kids did at Prestyn's party. Connor wouldn't hear Asha even if she were yelling.

The thing is, Asha has had years of experience with Connor, and not just from school. Sam's mom was always inviting Connor over, even though the only two things Sam and Connor had in common were living on the same street and having parents who worked at the same law firm. Sam's mom kept pushing the boys to play soccer together. That didn't happen, of course, but Connor was at all of Sam's birthdays until he was ten. And every year he did the exact same thing.

"Connor used to lick the frosting on Sam's birthday cake before it was even cut."

"He did not!" says Sloane. That's just what Sam's mom said the first time Asha told her. It's weird the way people want to deny this.

"He did it for three years in a row." After that first year, Asha watched Connor to know whether the cake was safe to eat. It never was until he stopped coming, and by that point there were so few guests, Sam didn't even have a proper cake. "I could never have the cake because of him."

"That's so sad," says Joanna, glancing up from her skyscraper sketch.

"It was sad," Asha agrees happily.

Sloane sighs, just like Sam's mom would. "Even if that's true, that was a really long time ago. He's changed."

"Exactly how?" asks Lexi.

"He's taller and cuter and better at soccer. He's grown up." Sloane gazes at him, and the other three girls follow. He is waving around a cupcake with shiny chocolate frosting as thick as a thatched roof.

"Oh, no," says Lexi.

Slowly, he peels down the paper wrapper.

"That frosting," says Asha. No good can come out of Connor having that much frosting.

"Shhhhh," says Sloane.

Connor turns it on its side and stuffs the entire thing, cake side first, in his mouth so that for a moment, the crown of frosting is exploding out. It looks like he's throwing up in reverse. Asha almost gags.

Then the cupcake is gone.

"Grown up, huh?" says Lexi.

"He's got personality. It just makes him cuter."

"Ugh," says Asha.

Joanna's nose is wrinkled, and she's shaking her head.

"Nice try, Sloanie. I think you're outvoted three to one."

Asha does the math. Lexi, Joanna, and her. For once, Asha is on the winning side.

Asha now looks forward to lunch—it's her chance to talk architecture with Joanna. Last week, Lexi asked Joanna why she likes buildings so much, and Joanna said, "I don't know, it's like each one is its own world," and Lexi said, "Huh?" but Asha understood exactly what she meant. Every building has its own unique feeling. Even supposedly identical ones have different light and shadows depending on where they're located. Like Donnybrooke—would it truly be the same if it didn't sit on the highest point in town?

"What kind of house do you live in?" Asha asks Joanna as she unzips her lunch box.

"I live in an apartment. Well, two apartments."

"Two? That's cool!"

Joanna shrugs. "It's just that one is my mom's and one is my dad's. And they're not big."

"But apartments are so cool. Are the rooms like this?" Asha puts her hands perpendicular to each other, but it's clear Joanna has no idea what she's talking about so Asha reaches for Joanna's sketchbook and pencil and says, "Can I?"

Joanna nods and hands them over.

Asha draws doors and then a layout, rectangles inside a rectangle.

"My mom's is mostly like that," says Joanna. She takes the sketchbook back and moves a couple of walls. "But my dad's is more like this," she says, adding on a sharply angled balcony, like half a trapezoid.

"That's in the building by the library!" It has to be from that shape.

"It is! Wow—you're good. You know, before I moved to Coreville, I lived in a building that was a cylinder and our apartment was shaped like a slice of pizza."

"So all the furniture was like the toppings?"

"That's what I used to think, too!"

Asha happily munches on some carrot sticks as Joanna keeps sketching buildings—first a tower that would have pizza-shaped apartments, then an apartment complex where the units are like unevenly stacked toy blocks. Then Joanna starts on something that is not an apartment building or a skyscraper or like anything else Joanna usually draws. It's far smaller. And, as it takes shape, far more familiar.

It's Donnybrooke.

Joanna captures the complicated roofline and the exact slant and shading of the different turrets. The only bit that's wrong is the weather vane, which, in her picture, is just a dash on top of a small rod. Asha's heart pounds with the memory of being there—and the memory of leaving. She forces herself to take a rose-and-candle breath.

"Do you recognize it?" Joanna asks.

Like that's even a question. "The weather vane—it's not a line."

"That's what it looks like from my apartment."

"It's an eagle trying to catch a fish. If you came over to my house, you could see it better." As soon as Asha says that, she realizes that she's invited Joanna over without even meaning to. And that she really hopes Joanna says yes.

When Joanna comes over after school on Thursday, she's way more interested in Asha's house than Donnybrooke, even though Asha just lives in a boring split-level with a medium-size yard. Joanna compliments the windows in the back and the swiveling lawn chairs and even the potted purple pansies that Asha's dad bought her mom for her birthday. But most of all, Joanna loves the trees. She tackles the sugar maple in the front yard with a flying leap, grabbing a branch and hoisting herself up. Before Asha can finish climbing her much smaller Japanese maple, Joanna jumps down with a laugh, neatly landing on both feet. Then she does the whole routine all over again. Asha had no idea that Joanna would be like this once she put her sketchbook away.

Asha perches on her favorite branch of her tree. "If you want a good view of Donnybrooke, you can climb the pine trees in the back. They're even higher."

"Higher?" says Joanna, landing on her feet a third time. "Great! Let's go." She takes off to the backyard.

Asha wants to join Joanna, and she will soon. Really soon, actually. She just needs a minute first. Because last week, on Thursday, in fact, she thought she saw Sam in his green Castleton polo turning off her street, Maplevale Lane, onto Oakstone Street, which just happens to link up to Hunt Place—the street Donnybrooke is on. She called for him, but he didn't reply. So then she texted him, asking if he's been on her street and if he wanted to kill her Househaunt monsters and what he was doing for Halloween. He didn't reply. She even asked her mom to text his mom to make sure everything was OK, but still—no reply.

Finally Asha texted Rohan, explaining the situation, and he responded, **A cry in the wilderness. So sorry!** when he should have said, **Sam's phone must have died.** Asha needed a better answer, so she FaceTimed Rohan and said, "I think maybe Sam is sick," because there had to be some reason that her best friend would just stop texting her altogether. Rohan said, "I don't think so," and Asha told him his beard looked really silly, and Rohan told her not to get mad at him when she was really mad at Sam for not replying. Which was not at all what Rohan should have said when he had no idea whether Sam was well or not.

But here Sam is, coming up the hill again, and he looks completely fine, which maybe should be a relief, but in reality, isn't.

"Sam! I texted you," Asha says. "A bunch of times. I need to talk to you about stuff." Before she can decide whether to start with Halloween or Househaunt, two more Castleton kids join him: Tessa, who's been friends with Prestyn forever, and a boy with short dark hair. So, Sam has made new friends at Castleton. Asha had figured as much, so she shouldn't be upset just because they're standing in front of her.

She takes a rose-and-candle breath and tries to be polite. "Hi, I'm Asha."

The boy starts laughing. The sound is as horribly unexpected and as instantly recognizable as the eagle-and-fish painting in the Donnybrooke foyer. "I know who you are. Considering I kicked you out of my house."

The words slice into Asha. It's true, the eyes are the same, blue and hard, and the nose is small and straight. "Prestyn?"

"Took you long enough."

"But your hair?" Asha can't help but touch her own.

"I cut it." Prestyn's wide smile reminds Asha of a crocodile. "Now we have nothing in common."

It's true. Without the hair, everything about them is different. Their skin, their eyes, even their teeth, thinks Asha as she rubs her tongue on her braces. And the bigger things, too. Their homes. Their friends. Their luck.

The knot in Asha's chest twists. She can feel a stress laugh rising beneath it, trying to escape. She beats it back.

It's Prestyn who laugh instead, a single hard beat. "Why are we even here? Sam?"

"We can go if you want."

"I want," says Prestyn.

Asha's urge to laugh flips into an urge to yell. "You're friends with her? Seriously?" she snaps.

Sam steps back and jams his hands in his pockets. He doesn't say anything, but he's obviously uncomfortable. Well, he should be. He should. It's not fair that he ignores Asha when Asha was his first real friend and went trick-or-treating with him every year and would always share the candy she got from the haunted houses he was too scared to approach and made him a planetarium umbrella and taught him how to really play

Househaunt and how to fake play soccer. And it's not fair Sam gets to visit Donnybrooke. He said he didn't even care about it, and now he's going over there and not even sticking up for her with Prestyn. Prestyn!

"You know what we used to call her."

Sam's head snaps up. For the first time since that party, he looks right at her. "Don't say it."

"You laughed so hard," says Asha. She can almost hear the sound of it, a bray like an overjoyed farm animal.

"Wait, are you guys talking about me?" says Prestyn.

"No," says Sam just as Asha says, "Yes."

It was soon after Asha's first time in Donnybrooke. Sam and Asha were at one of their early sessions with Ms. Summer, playing a rhyming game.

Sam goes first: "Sam. Bam, ram, lamb, am, ham, dam, jam, tram." He rocks it, as Rohan says.

Asha has an idea. "My name means hope, so I'm going to rhyme with that. Hope. Soap, nope, rope, dope, cope, pope, mope . . . Is *mope* a word?"

"Yes!" says Ms. Summer, opening the prize box.

"That's not fair," says Sam. "Her name is Asha, not Hope."

"But Asha isn't so good for rhyming," says Ms. Summer while Asha picks out a castle eraser.

When they get to Asha's car, Rohan is already in the back seat between their two booster seats. "Did you learn anything fun with Ms. Summer?" he asks.

"I learned my name was bad for rhyming," says Asha.

"That's not necessarily a bad thing," says Rohan.

"Yes, it is," says Asha.

"There's a kid in my science class named Gene, and his name rhymes with *gangrene*, which is this really gross disease where your skin—"

"That's enough," says Asha's dad.

"Well, his name also rhymes with *spleen*, and when we studied the human body, some mean kids called him Gene the Spleen."

"What's a spleen?" asks Asha.

"It's a body part you don't want your name to rhyme with," says Rohan as the car turns onto Coreville Avenue.

Asha thinks about this as she spots Donnybrooke, that amazing house that belongs to Prestyn Donaldson. Asha still isn't sure what she did wrong at that party, but whatever it was, Prestyn didn't have to be that mean about it, and make all her friends be mean, too. Because they were so, so mean.

It comes to Asha in a flash.

"Prestyn the Intestine," she announces to the car.

"Nice one!" Rohan raises his hand for a high five. Their dad can't seem to stop coughing in the front seat.

"Prestyn the Intestine. Prestyn the Intestine." Her chest feels lighter each time she says it. "Prestyn the Intestine."

Sam starts laughing. Asha has never heard Sam laugh like that before. It's a wonderful sound. He stops just long enough to say, "Intestines make poop!"

"They do!" says Asha. "Prestyn the Intestine!"

Asha's dad says, "While that's a clever rhyme, you should probably not say that. It's impolite."

"That girl deserves it." Rohan high-fives Sam and then Asha again.

"It's OK," says Asha. "She can't hear me."

But now, right now, if Asha says it, Prestyn will hear. Prestyn who gets to live in Donnybrooke and keeps her out and laughs at her and steals her friend. That Prestyn.

"Don't," says Sam, who has finally found something he'll talk to Asha about. His hands are shaking in his pockets. Serves him right.

Prestyn steps in front of him. "What did you used to call me?"

"Prestyn the Intestine," says Asha.

"What?"

Asha slows her speech down. "Prestyn. The. Intestine. Intestines make . . ."

She smiles at Sam, but he doesn't smile back. His mouth tightens in a flat line. Then he runs, just as fast as ever. Suddenly none of this seems funny.

"What, are we in, like, first grade?" says Tessa, rolling her eyes. She tugs at Prestyn's sleeve, and they follow Sam up Maplevale Lane.

So now, Prestyn doesn't just have a turreted bedroom and huge parties and a view of the whole of Coreville from her roof deck. She has Sam, too. Asha wonders how many times he's been over. At least two, but probably more. Three? Four? Five?

"What are you waiting for?"

Asha jumps. Joanna has appeared beside her. Asha had forgotten she was even over. Did she see what happened? Hear how stupid Asha sounded? Like Sam, does she wish she were friends with Prestyn instead?

But Joanna says, "It's so fun being here! Come climb in the backyard? Those trees are the best!"

Asha nods and runs hard to the back, where two white pines stand waiting for them. They are excellent trees to climb, both of them, and Sam has never tried, not even once. Asha starts up the taller white pine, leaving the thicker one for Joanna. Limb by limb, Asha climbs higher than she ever has before, higher than Sam could even dare imagine.

Sam

Sam wasn't even supposed to go to Prestyn's today. This was the day he was finally going to soccer club, like he was supposed to. Of course that's what he'd said to himself the last three Thursdays, but each time Prestyn asked him over to work on the Medieval Life project. He always said he had soccer, but then she always responded, "Can't you just skip it?" And it turns out, he actually could.

The first time he'd skipped, he'd actually planned to tell his parents the truth—that he missed soccer to work on a group project. After all, school came first even for them, right?

He didn't even consider lying until his mom opened the door with a huge smile and said, "Let's do dessert before dinner," and brought out a box of Coreville Farmcart cupcakes with soccer-ball frosting. She went on about how Sam was pushing himself and growing up and how the way he was taking on a challenge like soccer was such a great sign for his future. His dad—who would rather review a foot-high stack of contracts than so much as look at a soccer ball—said, "Great job!" and thanked him for being the reason he got a cupcake. It wasn't until they had their real dinner that his parents stopped talking enough to ask him how practice was, and Sam said, "Fine," and that was that. The next two Thursdays when he came home from Prestyn's, carefully timing his arrival to match when he'd get home on the activities bus, he didn't get cupcakes before dinner, but his parents were just as goofy and proud of him. He didn't want to ruin that.

And, to be honest, he didn't want to have to start going to soccer either. So what if it was supposed to be a club "for all skill levels, beginner to advanced"? It would still be miserable.

But this week, he'd turned in the Medieval Life project on Monday. So there was no reason to go to Prestyn's. He'd have to deal with soccer. Maybe his mom was right that he'd grown and all of that. Or maybe the four-letter boys would imagine a big circle on his back and use him as target practice. That seemed way more likely.

But then, on his way to lunch today, Prestyn said, "You're coming over after school, right?"

"Today?" he asked.

"Yes, today. Why? Do you want to go to soccer instead?"

He never *wanted* to go to soccer. And maybe it was coincidence, but since he started going to her house, he hadn't been called Miracle Boy once. And in science, kids no longer sighed dramatically if they were assigned to work with him, and in the cafeteria, they didn't scoot away like his lunch smelled bad. Sometimes kids even talked to him, not like he was their best friend, but not like he was invisible either.

"No," he said. "I want to go to your house."

But now that Asha has decided to go and call Prestyn that stupid old nickname from way back when, he wonders if going to Donnybrooke was the right choice. His afternoon might have been easier if he were facing Alec and the four-letter gang instead of an angry Prestyn. Yes, he had laughed. Yes, he had said it, too. But that was way before he went to Castleton. Way before he actually knew Prestyn. He would never, ever call her that now.

Prestyn doesn't even speak to him when she gets to the gate. She just taps in the code and slides right by him. The crested doors slowly creak open, and Sam watches their shadow cross his own. He imagines them as a time-space portal that, once closed, will trap you forever.

"Coming?" asks Tessa.

And he does because he knows his thoughts are too silly to listen to.

Prestyn keeps ignoring him once they're inside. Sam puts all his stuff in the front closet and then, alone, stares at the eagle-and-fish painting in the foyer. He shivers. The fish has its mouth open like it's gulping air. But it's a fish. Air would drown it.

"Did you really call me that?" Prestyn calls from the hallway.

Would a fish breathing air feel the same as a human breathing water?

"Did you?"

Would it feel worse than the eagle grabbing it? There's so little space between those talons and the fish's skin.

"That's kind of a gross thing to call someone, don't you think? Don't you?"

Sam forces himself into the hallway where the girls are. "It was just because it rhymed."

"Wow! You're such a poet," says Prestyn.

"So original," says Tessa, echoing that same sarcastic tone.

"Whose stupid idea was it anyway?" asks Prestyn.

"Asha's," says Sam. Well, it was.

"At least it wasn't you," says Tessa. "Let's get a snack."

Sam follows the girls into the kitchen and tries not to think about eagles and fish. As usual, the girls get out chips and guacamole, which only Tessa seems to eat, and a bowl of M&M's. Prestyn picks out a blue one to suck on. Sam wishes his parents let him have M&M's whenever he wanted them. Although he's not actually sure if Prestyn's parents are OK with it. They're never here when he is.

"Do your parents know I'm over?"

Prestyn loudly swallows what's left of her M&M. "Of course they do. I made sure to tell my mom before we even started working on the castle."

"So, it's OK?"

"We had a school project together. What are they going to say? Anyway, it's my house, too. It's not like they get to control everything I do here."

"I just wanted to make sure since they're never around."

"How can you even say that? Besides, my dad has to travel a lot. For work. And if you stayed a little later, you'd meet my mom. I'm sure she'd totally love that. Or you can go over to your friend Asha's house if you'd like it better there."

That stops Sam's questions. He shouldn't have asked them in the first place. The problem is, he's not sure what he should say. Everything he's tried has come out wrong.

"So, did you and Asha go out?"

Sam doesn't even realize Tessa is talking to him until she asks the question again.

"What?" he says.

"You and Asha. Were you like boyfriend-girlfriend? She *likes* you, doesn't she?"

"No," he says. Asha just wants everything to be like it was when they were little. That's what his mom told him, and she's right.

"You brought her to my party," says Prestyn.

"My dad told me to," says Sam. He's telling the truth, but this conversation is making his stomach feel funny. That and the smell of the guacamole.

"She got all smiley with you," says Tessa.

"She smiles at everyone."

"Asha never smiles at me," says Prestyn.

"She smiles at everyone who's nice to her," clarifies Sam. Tessa giggles, but it's true. Asha is always nice to whoever is nice to her. Not like Prestyn, who picks and chooses. When Prestyn is nice to him, it reminds him of when he got accepted to Castleton. Not everyone is so lucky.

Sam takes out his phone while Prestyn and Tessa whisper-giggle over the candy bowl. He hasn't played Househaunt in a while, and his master bedroom is rattling. That means Bed-Thugs. And that means he'll need to back them into a hot dryer if he wants to get rid of them for good. He grabs a torch and gets to work. It only takes a minute for him to drive them down into the basement. He hasn't lost his monster-killing touch.

He angles carefully to the washer-dryer. It's squelchier than he remembered.

Wait! That squelch was not the dryer. It's a Zombie-Self. He needs to work fast. He jabs the torch at the Bed-Thugs, backing them in. But one crawls out of the dryer just as a Zombie-Self enters the laundry room.

"Do you want to play a game?" asks Prestyn, her voice right behind him.

Sam almost drops his phone.

"What?" he asks, fumbling to recover.

"Do. You. Want. To. Play. A. Game."

As she's talking, his phone lets out a little shriek. He's dead. He hopes it was the Bed-Thugs. He's always hated the idea of being killed by a cold, brainless version of himself.

"You made me die," he says.

"No, I didn't," laughs Prestyn. She looks at his phone. "And you have what? Four more lives?"

He does. Which is quite a lot and he could earn more. So maybe it's OK.

"Besides, it's not very social of you to be on your phone." Prestyn sounds just like his mom, which is really weird. "We could play hide-and-seek," Prestyn says with a little smile.

Sam gets it. It's a big joke. Hide-and-seek is for little kids.

"If you want," says Tessa. "You only have to play if you want."

"Tessa! You said you were bored, remember? You want Sam to play, too. And you love hide-and-seek."

"That's true, I do. It's just I don't know if Sam . . ."

"Of course he wants to play! This is the best house ever for hide-and-seek. Come on, Sam, you'll see." Prestyn flashes Sam a grin.

Sam slides off his bar stool and follows the girls to the elevator at the center of the house. It's a relief that girls like Prestyn and Tessa still like to play a game like hide-and-seek, something simple that he actually knows. He must have played a hundred times with Asha, back when they were hanging out. She loved hiding. Once she curled up in a suitcase in a storage closet, and another time she climbed in a hamper and threw clothes on top of herself. It could take half an hour to find her if she stayed quiet. Sam wonders how long it would take to find someone in a house this size.

With a whine and a bump, the elevator lands on the main floor. Prestyn opens the door, then the inner gate. Its mirrored walls don't hide the fact that it's smaller than any elevator Sam has ever been in. Of course it's the only one he's ever seen in a house, so that's pretty cool. Almost as cool as a planetarium in a school.

"Ground rules," says Prestyn as she steps in.

Sam listens up. He's all in favor of some rules.

"First, no hiding in my parents' offices or their room or my room or any bathrooms, of course."

Sam is in complete agreement, but still his face feels hot at the mention of all those private spaces.

"And whoever is It has to count to thirty. Slowly. If you come down too soon, you have to go back on the roof deck and be It all over again."

Sam stops. "The roof deck?"

"Yeah. The roof deck. That's where you count," says Prestyn.

That's not going to work. He can't be stuck on the roof deck, the highest point in Coreville, way higher than all the trees he never climbs.

"What's the problem?" asks Tessa.

Sam stares down into the gap between the elevator and the main floor. The darkness goes on and on. "I can't be It," he blurts.

"That's not fair," says Prestyn.

"I don't like heights," Sam says.

"You like outer space," says Tessa. "That's as high as it gets."

That is not a fair comparison. Thinking about outer space in your head is completely different from having your feet on a roof deck with a flimsy railing and the whole town below it. Especially since in space, the force of gravity isn't trying to make you fall down. "I really, really don't like heights."

The elevator buzzes grumpily as it waits.

"Fine, fine, just get in!" says Prestyn, and Sam does. "OK, since it's your first time playing, Tessa can be It. But then it's normal hide-and-seek rules."

"OK," says Sam. It *is* OK for this one game, and that's more than he was expecting.

When the elevator gets to the top of the house, the girls step off while Sam stays on. Even from inside it, Sam spies the swaying treetops and, farther on, the uneven lines of carved-up neighborhoods. His knees wobble a little. Yes, he still hates heights.

Prestyn whispers something to Tessa, then steps back into the elevator and presses a button.

"I can't believe you and that girl Asha would call me that," says Prestyn as the elevator descends. "Like, what did I ever do to you?"

Sam jams his hands in his pockets. His legs twitch. They want to run, but he is stuck in the smallest possible space with nowhere to go. He bounces in place until the elevator comes to a stop with a light thud. They're in the basement.

"Anyway, whatever," says Prestyn, walking off. "I have the perfect hiding place for you."

In front of them is a dimly lit glass room, filled with racks of bottles. Even though its walls are almost close enough to touch, it reminds Sam of the light from cool and distant stars.

"The wine cellar," says Prestyn. "The best hiding place in the house."

"It's glass," says Sam.

Prestyn rolls her eyes. "If you go behind the racks, it's dark enough that no one can find you."

She leads him to the back. It's a little chilly inside, like when you step outside on the first cool day of fall, but Prestyn is right. Between the dimness and the floor-to-ceiling racks filled with wine bottles, it's a great hiding place.

"Thanks," says Sam.

"Just keep it dark in here until Tessa finds you. Don't turn on your phone or anything. Unless you want to be It."

Sam doesn't want to be It. He's not going to give up yet.

But he is cold.

At first, the coldness didn't bother him much, even in his short sleeves. But he's been in here a really long time. If he could check his phone, he would know exactly how long. He did try running in place, but the wine bottles shook, so he's left rubbing his arms and blowing on his hands. It's not enough to keep him warm. And he's beginning to get worried that he might be late getting home. He decides to take a very quick peek at his phone, just to check the time. It's 4:52.

What's taking Tessa so long? She's been to this house a lot. She must know all the hiding places. But there are so many. And she's starting from the top of the house.

He checks his phone again, but fast. 4:56. This is the time he likes to leave. Actually, one minute after. But he can stay a few more minutes if he runs all the way home instead of walks. He'd like to win this. It would be nice to beat Castleton kids at something, even if it is only hide-and-seek. He checks again. 4:58. His fingernails look bluish, but maybe that's the light in here. He could text Prestyn, tell her he has to go. But then she'd know that he's been on his phone. He doesn't want to break the rules of the one game he's been invited to play. And he really doesn't want to be It next time. If there is a next time.

He knows what to do. He'll count to a hundred. Then he'll go, no matter what. One, two, three . . .

. . . ninety-nine, one hundred. OK, he'll go. He presses his numb fingers extra hard against the phone to check it one last time. 5:00. He makes his way to the front of the wine cellar. He really is late.

The door opens. Warm air and Prestyn's voice rush in. "I told you not to check your phone. The light totally gave it away."

"I have to go now. I'm late," he says, pushing past her. He can picture his mom waiting by the front door.

"You should have come up then," says Tessa.

"Yeah," says Prestyn, following him into the elevator. "It's not like we locked you in."

In the mirrored walls, the girls are smiling at each other. The way their reflection goes on and on makes Sam almost as dizzy as the roof deck does.

"Well, at least you won't be It next time," says Prestyn.

Next time. She said it, not him. There is going to be a next time. That's all Sam can think about as he sprints out the crested gate, past Asha's house, across Coreville Avenue, through his neighborhood to his house. He's invited back even without a school project. He unlocks his front door, drops his stuff, and collapses on the couch to catch his breath. He's the first one home.

His mom walks in two minutes later, holding a large Coreville Farmcart grocery bag in her arms.

"Must have been quite a practice," she says. "You still seem winded."

Asha

Asha can't help but smile as she sticks a cutout At-tick Fana-tick on her haunted house costume, because not only is it Halloween, it's Thursday, too, and Asha saw Prestyn walking home from the bus stop by herself, no Sam in sight. No one came home with Asha either, but Joanna will be over to give out candy with her. So even though it was totally rude for Sam and his mom not to reply about their plans, she's not going to spend Halloween alone.

The sun is still bright, but Asha is ready. Her dad has carved the jack-o'-lanterns, her mom has filled three cauldron-shaped candy bowls (plus a small prize bowl for kids who can't eat candy), and Asha has decked out the front yard in cobwebs and a supersized inflatable black cat. She has even FaceTimed Rohan to show him her costume. He answered wearing the same Yoda ears he's had for the past six Halloweens and told her she "epitomized the ethos of All Hallows' Eve," which apparently was a big compliment. So, the costume, candy, and decorations are set. The only things missing are the trick-or-treaters and Joanna.

A red hatchback pulls up to the curb, and out pops a Statue of Liberty, complete with a coppery green face, book, and torch. She waves at Asha, who has to squint for a second before she says, "Joanna? Is that you?"

"It's Liberty-me."

"Wow!"

"Well, you're a haunted house! That's amazing! I didn't even think about being a building."

"But the Statue of Liberty is a building, too. A really cool one, actually."

"I guess it is—thanks." Joanna points to Asha's sleeve with her torch. "What's that?"

"A Screech-Leech. I've got the other monsters, too, but this arm is all Screech-Leeches," Asha says, stretching it out.

Joanna shakes her head. "Screech-Leech?"

"You know, from Househaunt."

"What's Househaunt?"

"You don't play Househaunt?"

Joanna shakes her head again.

"Never?" Asha knows not every kid plays Househaunt, maybe

not even most, but this game was made for Joanna. Asha runs inside to get her phone. When she returns, she pulls up all the easy-mode house choices and hands her phone to Joanna to pick one. After a bit of scrolling, Joanna settles on a skinny town house with a large bay window.

"So look at it carefully," Asha says, "because then this picture is going to go away and you'll have to build it from the inside. And if you put in the wrong kind of room or stairway or whatever, monsters will appear, and if you don't keep it clean, monsters will appear, and if your house has way, way too many monsters, it will be condemned."

"Condemned, like you die?"

"No. It's worse than dying." That's true, and not just because you get seven lives in this game and you can earn more as you go, so dying usually just means your corpse turns into a Zombie-Self. Being condemned means that your house has to live forever with your monsters, and it's not even worth trying to clean it because it's a lost cause. It's worse than dead. Sometimes, when Asha feels her absolute worst, when her whole world is too much and it's hard to breathe or see or think, she wonders if that's what it's like to be condemned. But in the end, that feeling always goes away. Being condemned is forever.

"Is being condemned really gross? I hate gross games."

"I've never been condemned." Asha isn't trying to brag, but

she is an excellent Househaunt player. Even at the hardest level, she rarely makes a mistake in constructing her house. She only sprouts monsters when Rohan and Sam aren't around to maintain her properties, but they always get to it soon enough. At least they always have so far.

"I guess I'll try," says Joanna. But just as she's about to hit play, a little ladybug, dinosaur, and cat come running up, plastic pumpkins rattling with their first few pieces of candy. As soon as Asha and Joanna hand them more, a pirate and bumblebee are at their heels yelling, "Trick or treat!" followed by a piglet so small she has to be carried. After that, the stream doesn't stop. Maplevale Lane always attracts kids from all over Coreville because the houses have the spookiest decorations and the families give out the most candy. Joanna says hi to a few dragons and butterflies she knows from her apartment building.

As the night wears on, there are fewer animals and more Darth Vaders and Black Panthers. By the time the kids are bigger than she is, Asha is ready to be done. She pours all the remaining candy into one big cauldron and wonders whether Sam went trick-or-treating after all.

"Are those your friends?" asks Joanna.

Asha gulps and turns. A gaggle of girls are coming up the walk, each in their own color of neon spandex, with small, slanted hats like the tips of highlighter pens. Behind them are boys, all wearing sandwich boards made to look like notebook pages with highlighted text.

"Trick or treat," says the blue highlighter girl.

It's Prestyn. Asha knows from her voice. She doesn't have to look at her face. Another sandwich-board boy steps out from the shadows and puts his hands on Prestyn's shoulders. It's not Sam. Asha scans the faces of the rest of the boys.

"Where's Sam?" she asks.

Prestyn laughs. "Not with you obviously."

"He's not with you either."

"Not at the moment." Prestyn points a perfectly manicured blue fingernail at Asha. "You're supposed to be giving us candy, not grilling us about your ex-friend."

What does Prestyn mean by that? Asha and Sam are still friends. Things are just a little weird right now.

Prestyn sighs dramatically. "I guess we'll just have to help ourselves." In a flash of blue, Prestyn grabs the candy cauldron and holds it high over her head. "Who wants candy?"

"Give it back!" says Asha as highlighter girls and notebook-paper boys call, "Me! Me!"

Prestyn smirks as she tosses handfuls into her friends' bags. She's taking every last piece!

"Stop it!" yells Asha. "Stop it!" She grabs Joanna's torch and points it right at Prestyn.

"Take a chill pill," Prestyn says, and drops the bowl. There's only a few Jolly Ranchers and a KitKat left. "Let's find a house where no one is going to freak out on us." As the group heads off, Asha hears someone imitate her "Stop it!"

Asha's face feels hot. Why did she have to yell like that? She knows it was too loud. And she snatched Joanna's torch without even asking. But Prestyn was so mean about Sam and then she started taking all the candy. All of it! But still, Joanna must think she's really weird. And the evening had been going so well. Joanna had even loved her costume.

Asha hears the crinkle of a wrapper.

"Do you want it?" Joanna is holding half the KitKat bar out to her.

Asha shakes her head. She's not hungry, even if it does smell good. The highlighter girls are across the street, but she can still hear their giggles.

"She's really not your friend," says Joanna.

"No. She's not." Asha turns around. Over the back of her house and up the hill, Donnybrooke's weather vane sits on its turret, backlit by the moon. "That's her house, you know."

Joanna nods solemnly, just like a Statue of Liberty should. "I'm not surprised. It looks like the kind of house a mean girl would live in."

"It does?" says Asha. What does Joanna mean by that? That it's fancy? But that's not Donnybrooke's fault.

"It does to me. Here, let's split it," says Joanna, offering the KitKat to Asha again. This time she takes it. Asha thinks about Joanna's words as she chews the chocolate, and then again as she gets ready for bed. Asha has always believed she would be an altogether different girl if she were waking up in Donnybrooke each day instead of watching it from her back window, if her eyes blinked open to a telescoping turret instead of her flat ceiling. And if every afternoon, instead of walking to her ordinary house by herself, she went home to Donnybrooke and all the kids in her class wished they could go with her. She doesn't think that it would make her mean.

But she is sure that it would make her lucky.

Donnybrooke the Mansion
with a Ghastly Halloween Tale

Halloween is something of a tricky night. It's hard not to be a little envious when the children approach all the ordinary houses in town with such delight while they ignore Donnybrooke. It's like a couple of jack-o'-lanterns and some fake cobwebs count for more than multiple turrets and a portico. Of course it may not be entirely the children's fault. Mrs. Donaldson prefers to keep the gates closed, though she does always hire an old babysitter of Prestyn's to hand out candy to anyone who makes it that far down the cul-de-sac.

Nevertheless, Halloween inside Donnybrooke is something of a treat. Mrs. Donaldson always hosts a lovely pre-trick-or-treating get-together for Prestyn, and this year, thankfully, was no exception. Tessa, Olivia C., Olivia D., Olivia E., Elle, and Addison all came over to get dressed up. When they were done, everyone agreed that Prestyn, in a neon blue that made her eyes shine, was the cutest of the bunch (well, everyone except Addison, but what do you expect from the little snit?). They admired Prestyn, they admired Donnybrooke, and it was just what a party should be.

But then Mrs. Donaldson made a curious comment about boys coming over, which was strange because Donnybrooke wasn't expecting Sam. But then again, Donnybrooke never really expects Sam and he's there every Thursday.

The doorbell rang.

The gates opened.

It was not Sam.

It was Alec the Stair Destroyer! And each and every one of his guacamole-smearing, mansion-abusing minions! The Donaldsons leave the pumpkins and candy bowls outside the gates only to let the hooligans in? Prestyn and Mrs. Donaldson didn't even blink when the boys slid down the banisters and sat on the granite counters. It was like the Night of Mayhem and Stair Destruction hadn't ever happened. Alec, crude as ever, left a handful of blue corn chips in the powder room toilet. On the bright side, at least *that* misdeed could be flushed away. (Meanwhile, the roof deck stairs are still boarded up.) Luckily all of the children left for trick-or-treating before more serious damage could occur.

Still, perplexing.

Why would Mrs. Donaldson approve of those hooligans while disapproving of the boy who always remembers to put his water glass in the sink? Granted, he made one unfortunate comment, but since then he has only treated her mansion with the utmost courtesy. Donnybrooke hates to question her judgment, but . . . perhaps, in this one limited matter, it is questioning her judgment.

After the children left, Donnybrooke searched for Sam as far as it could see. It saw Asha doling out candy, and Prestyn leading her pack. The boy, however, could not be found.

Well, at least it was a decent night for Donnybrooke. The worst damage it suffered was some Coreville Farmcart salsa on its counters, and at least that's the priciest salsa in town. Organic, too. There might have been a time when Donnybrooke would have complained about spills, but after the last "party," it understands how much worse it could be. On the whole, it and its family were admired and appreciated, and at the center of this evening's festivities right where they belong. To be sure, it might have been even better if Mr. Donaldson were there, but once he hears how well it went, he's sure to make more of an effort next time. After all, even he can't resist being on a winning team.

Now the night is over. Prestyn, the star of the evening, is

sleeping soundly under her turret. The only trace of her costume is the neon blue on her nails. The rest of her, from the big toe sticking out of her duvet to her head heavy on her pillow, is the girl Donnybrooke has always known and always loved, breathing in her mansion's air, restoring herself for another day.

Asha

The worst part of seeing Dr. Shirazi is not the awkward questions she asks about how Asha is doing in school, and socially, and with her medication. It's not that Asha has to eat her snack in the car in the rush to make it on time, or the fact that Asha is pretty sure that she will have to see Dr. Shirazi for-absolutely-ever. It's not that Asha has to have those appointments in addition to the ones with her psychologist, Dr. Wells. It's not even that she can't have Joanna over this Thursday. The worst part of seeing Dr. Shirazi is that no one else has to.

Yes, Asha's mom says that there's a wait list to get in to see her, and Dr. Shirazi says she has seen thousands of kids in her years of practice as a child psychiatrist, but Asha doesn't know any of those people. Asha is quite sure Joanna doesn't see her. And that Lexi doesn't. And that Sloane doesn't. They don't have any of the appointments that Asha has had as long as she can remember. Sam was the only one who did, but Asha is pretty sure even he doesn't anymore. He goes to Prestyn's. Or at least he did before Halloween.

Asha munches on a few pretzel sticks as she and her mom wait at the stoplight at Maplevale Lane and Coreville Avenue. Before it changes, the Castleton Academy bus pulls up, and Asha can't help but watch as the kids file off, teeny-tiny, then small, then Sam, which doesn't make sense since this isn't his stop and he isn't good enough friends with Prestyn to go trick-or-treating with her. But here he is, waiting around as the medium-size kids get off and then the big kids, like Prestyn and Tessa. Once the bus leaves, Sam does his butterfly walk with stops and starts. Still, it's clear. He's going home with Prestyn.

Maybe watching Sam follow Prestyn is actually the worst part of going to Dr. Shirazi's.

The best part about going to Dr. Shirazi is that when it's over, Asha's mom always takes her to Coreville Farmcart, which is next door. According to Asha's mom, way back before people had computers and microwaves, there used to be an actual cart set up there that sold goods from local farms. Now it's a grocery store that has hand-dipped chocolates and gelato flavors you can't find anywhere else, and it's much too expensive to shop at every week. The only time Asha and her mom go is after Dr. Shirazi. If her mom is in the right mood, Asha can even convince her to take a pint of overpriced gelato home.

Today, as Asha turns down the freezer aisle, she checks out the fall gelato flavors—caramel apple, cranberry-pomegranate, and, of course, pumpkin spice. Too sweet, too tart, and too blah. Even her dad would be sad if she came home with one of those flavors. She'll have to rely on the classics. As she searches for just the right chocolate, not too dark and not too chunky, she spots someone with a blond bun on the other end of the aisle moving backward. It's such a strange sight, even stranger when she realizes that someone is Sam's mom. And she is about to—

CRASH!

Sam's mom backs straight into a display of ice-cream cones. The boxes tumble around her in a pastel flurry.

From nowhere, Asha's mom appears. "Are you all right, Cassie?"

"I'm fine, just fine." A Farmcart employee rushes over and starts restacking the boxes. "Wow! It's so unexpected to see you two here!" says Sam's mom.

It is unexpected. Almost as unexpected as her walking backward down the freezer aisle. But not quite as unexpected as her not returning any of Asha's mom's texts.

"Did Sam go trick-or-treating?" asks Asha.

Sam's mom makes a small O before she smiles just with the sides of her mouth like she's about to floss her back teeth.

"I'm so sorry about not getting back to you, Divya," she says to Asha's mom. "It's just been so busy with Sam starting Castleton."

"Of course, no worries," says Asha's mom in a fake-friendly voice.

"Did he go trick-or-treating?" asks Asha again.

"Asha!" says her mom in a whisper loud enough for anyone in the freezer aisle to hear.

Sam's mom presses her lips together. Two ice-cream cone boxes have been restacked on either side of her head so it looks like she's sprouted horns.

"He didn't. He decided he was getting too old for it. I guess that's what happens as kids grow up. They move on. That's what we hope for at least, right?"

"Of course," says Asha's mom, though her voice suddenly sounds mad. She is holding on to her cart so hard that her knuckles pop up like cartoon muscles. "Asha didn't trick-or-treat either. She and a friend gave out candy."

"How nice! You're making new friends." Sam's mom uses a sticky-sweet voice like Asha is in first grade. Asha doesn't remember Sam's mom sounding like that when she actually was in first grade. "Sam is, too. Would you believe after all the fuss he used to make about soccer, he's playing intramural soccer as we speak?"

"What?" says Asha.

"He plays after school on Thursdays."

"What? No!" Asha is not trying to get him in trouble. But Sam does not play soccer after school on Thursdays.

"Oh, Asha, he's changed," Sam's mom says. She waves good-bye and turns around so quickly Asha doesn't even have time to decide what she wants to say back.

When Asha gets in the car, she turns up the radio. Even though it's on the pop station, which her mom usually finds annoying, she doesn't ask Asha to turn to public radio or the two classic rock stations. She gives Asha the space to listen to whatever she wants. Finally, when the station cuts to commercial, Asha switches off the radio and says, "Sam's mom used to like that I was friends with Sam."

"You're so right. I wish you had reminded her."

"Really? I thought that would be rude."

"Maybe it would be." Asha's mom sighs. "But it's just so true."

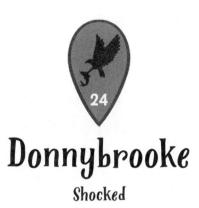

Donnybrooke

Shocked

Hide-and-seek is perhaps Donnybrooke's favorite game. It allows its guests to appreciate its intricacies in a way almost no other activity does, save a house tour. And hide-and-seek seems to remind Prestyn that she's the princess of this mansion, which makes her so happy. Indeed, she's grinning as she circles the living room, closing in on the boy.

"You're It!" she says.

He goes still at her words, even stiller than when he was hiding.

"Up you go," she says, her perfect teeth gleaming. Mrs. Donaldson certainly knew what she was doing when she picked out her orthodontist. Dr. Obi was worth every penny.

The boy stays wedged between the high-backed Italian leather sofa and the elegantly painted wall.

"Fine, I'll find Tessa first. But then you're It." Prestyn positively prances off.

Donnybrooke is a touch surprised the boy was caught first. His hiding place was one of the best in the house, far better than Tessa's behind the glass sunroom door. But then again, what does a mansion like Donnybrooke know about staying out of sight?

"So, you have to stay on the roof deck while you count," Prestyn says as she presses the topmost elevator button.

The boy takes a step back so that he is half off, half on the elevator. The doors won't shut with him like that.

"What?" says Prestyn, opening her eyes extra wide. She does look so winsome like that. "These are just the rules. And if Tessa and I are the only ones playing by them, well, that's just not fair." Her voice rises at the end, like it does whenever she asks her mother or father for a particularly special gift.

And just like her parents, the boy doesn't say no. He inches forward toward Prestyn and Tessa, so that when the elevator doors close, they just clear his back.

When the elevator stops at the top, the boy steps off first. His eyes dart toward the sky. He looks surprised at the coming twilight, as if he's forgotten the clocks have moved back an hour over the weekend. He shudders as he lets his eyes rest on the magnificent eagle-and-fish weather vane. He doesn't look down, not at the town below, not at the cracks in the deck under his feet.

Prestyn returns to the rules. "So, whoever is counting stands away from the elevator and slowly counts to forty."

"It was thirty," says the boy, almost cutting her off.

"No, it was forty. At least that's what I counted to. And Tessa, too, right?"

"Uh . . . I can't really remember, actually," says Tessa.

"It was forty, Tessa," says Prestyn.

"It was? I . . . um . . . OK. Yeah. Forty." Tessa is such a loyal friend, but she is a painfully terrible liar. The truth is, she didn't make it to ten. And Prestyn didn't count at all. Though as the hostess, surely she had her reasons.

She cocks her head at the boy, as if waiting for his challenge. It doesn't come.

"Forty," she says again, pointing. "Over there." Then she and Tessa make their escape.

The boy is honest. At first he rushes, onetwothreefour, but then he stops himself. He takes a deep breath. He starts over and counts just like Prestyn said he should. One. Two. Three. Four. He jogs in tight circles in the middle of the deck where

the boarded-up trap door holds the useless stairs. The girls get off the elevator in the basement. They enter the utility room, and then . . .

Oh!

Oh, dear!

Donnybrooke . . . Donnybrooke was not expecting that.

The boy finishes counting, unaware. He races to the elevator and pushes the down button.

Nothing happens.

He does it again. Still, nothing.

He presses it over and over, hard, then harder. He starts jabbing it so hard, his finger must hurt. Then, all at once, he stops and rubs his bare arms. He dashes over to the trap door, apparently unaware of the state of the stairs. He yanks at a board, but the Donaldsons have made sure it won't give. Just like Prestyn has now done with the elevator.

But why? Why flip that switch? The Donaldsons are supposed to make Donnybrooke more powerful, not less. They're all a team, aren't they? Whatever games the girls are playing aren't going to make the boy admire Donnybrooke. There's nothing impressive about a home that can't do what it was built to do. Surely Prestyn knows this. Hasn't she been taught the same lessons Donnybrooke has?

The boy shuffles back to the elevator and presses the button like he already knows it's a waste of energy. *It's not my fault*, Donnybrooke wants to tell him.

Suddenly the boy explodes, yelling and banging at the door. The noise echoes in the dusk, loud enough for all the houses down the hill to hear. The trees rouse, rustling their branches. They hiss about how terrible it is that boy is stuck, how Donnybrooke should do something. And for once, Donnybrooke agrees with them. It doesn't want the boy out here any more than they do. It tries to stretch and pull, but the elevator doors don't budge. It would open them if it could, but it can't. Mrs. Donaldson once said to Prestyn, "Can't or won't?" when Prestyn insisted she couldn't wear pinchy heels to cotillion. This is can't.

The boy runs to the other side of the roof deck. "Help!" he yells. "Help!"

He doesn't realize that Donnybrooke is literally powerless to help. But surely Prestyn and Tessa will. Soon, soon. There must be some explanation for their actions that a simple mansion like Donnybrooke happens to be unaware of.

A fat tear falls from the boy's face. He yells again into the swirling breeze.

Inside the utility room, the two girls giggle.

Asha

Asha is pretty sure that if it weren't for the whole thing with Sam's mom, she'd be stuck inside doing homework. But instead, almost as soon as they got home, her mom asked her if she'd like to decorate the outside with Diwali lights before the sun fully sets.

Asha said no at first because she knew her mom was just trying to distract her from the disaster at Coreville Farmcart. At least her mom didn't try to have a big conversation about it, but still, doing something fun is a lot less fun if you've been asked to do it just because people feel sorry for you. But then her mom said that she really could use the help, that Diwali was coming up, and that Asha would have no problem doing her homework later. Asha wasn't sure whether to believe all that—other than Diwali coming up, which is obviously true—but she knew it would make her mom feel better if she agreed. And there *is* something special about wrapping the strands of lights around the tree branches and transforming them into something festive. She loves that they stay up all the way to the new year. Sam once asked her if her favorite part of celebrating both Christmas and Diwali was all the presents, but really it's the lights, like stars on earth, that last for months.

As Asha climbs higher into the Japanese maple, a coil of lights hanging from her arm, she can't help but wonder what her mom would have suggested if she knew the truth—that instead of being at soccer, Sam is at Donnybrooke. Her mom probably would have let Asha have that Farmcart chocolate gelato for dinner. But it wouldn't even taste that good, thinking about Sam and Prestyn together, and her parents being worried about her, with every bite.

Sam's mom, though. How can she not know where he is? And how can she think Sam loves soccer? No matter how much Sam changes, Asha is sure he will always hate soccer. Although, before Sam got into Castleton, Asha would have said that no matter what happens, Sam would never be friends with Prestyn Donaldson, and he's over at her house right now. So maybe Sam's mom is right that he's changed, at least in some ways.

But, Asha realizes as she hears yelling in the distance, there's something about Sam that definitely hasn't changed.

His voice.

Sam

Sam's throat hurts from yelling, and tears sting his face.
As if it wasn't bad enough that they leaked out in the first place.
As if it wasn't even worse that he came up here in his uniform
polo without his jacket or his phone. But he was only supposed
to be up here for a minute. Not even.

The sun is dropping low. It's so much darker than when he's
usually over at Prestyn's. He knows the clocks have changed, but
even so, it's got to be around 5:00. And who knows how much
longer he'll be up here.

The deck under his feet feels as unstable as the swaying tops
of the trees. He tried looking up instead of out, but that's where
the weather vane is. It really is enormous up close. And that

eagle is intense, like something from a nightmare. No wonder Asha can't stop talking about it.

He ducks into the vestibule of the elevator and leans against it to steady himself. Why hasn't Prestyn come up yet? Or even Tessa? Aren't they wondering where he is? Don't they know he has to go? He should have left already. He closes his eyes, but that makes his head spin even worse. His insides start rumbling.

Except . . . it's not his insides. It's the elevator.

He turns around, and as he hears it stop, he tests the door. He almost falls into the opening gate and Prestyn.

"What took you so long?" she demands, rubbing the spot where Sam's nose connected with her head. "If you weren't going to play, you should have just said so. Tessa and I waited forever. She's gone home already."

The warmth of the elevator makes Sam's arms itch, and Prestyn's words don't make sense. He tried so hard to get down.

"I was stuck," he says.

"Really? Huh. Did you maybe press the button too hard and jam it? Or maybe there's something weird going on with our elevator. I'll have to tell my parents."

Is that possible? That the elevator broke? That somehow he broke it? But the button kept moving in and out. It didn't feel jammed.

"You look cold," says Prestyn. "Do you want some hot chocolate?"

Sam hesitates.

Prestyn flashes her cell phone at him. It's 4:59. "Oh, but I guess you don't have time."

In the elevator mirrors, her face is shining, strangely happy.

Asha

As Asha runs up Hunt Place, the only sounds she hears are coming from herself—her footsteps, her breathing, her heart. Sam has gone quiet. But there is one more sound now. A slow creak, the kind that pulls at your nerves. The gates of Donny-brooke are opening.

Asha jumps behind a trash can left out on the curb. The thought hits her with full force: She shouldn't be here. She promised she wouldn't. Who knows what Prestyn or Mrs. Donaldson would do if they found her? It's that question that keeps Asha behind the Donaldsons' trash can even though their garbage smells just as bad as everyone else's.

Bam. Bam. Bam. Hard footsteps, then a figure flies past. But it's not Mrs. Donaldson. It's not any Donaldson.

"Sam!" Asha calls, popping out from her hiding place.

He stops and stares at her in the near darkness. He's shivering, and he looks smaller than usual, as if something has been sucked out of him.

"Are you OK?" asks Asha.

"Why are you here?"

"You were yelling for help." He was. Over and over. She's not sure why he doesn't seem happier to see her. Behind him, the Donnybrooke gates creak closed.

"You heard me? From your house?"

"I was outside. And I heard you up on the roof. Weren't you on the roof deck?"

"Yeah," says Sam. But he doesn't explain or thank her or do any of the things she thought he would. Asha almost feels like she imagined the whole thing, him stuck up there in his green Castleton shirt, the long shadow of the weather vane behind him.

"Was the fish more sad or scared? I want the fish to be scared. Because then it still might get away. If it's sad, it means it knows it's going to get eaten."

Sam's teeth chatter out loud. "I need to go home. I'm late," he says, and starts to run.

"Your mom doesn't know you're here," Asha calls after him.

Sam stops in his tracks. "Don't tell her. Please." Then he sprints off, leaving Asha even more confused than she was in the grocery store with Sam's mom. It feels like that was weeks, not hours, ago.

A car drives up and slows down. Asha is trapped between its headlights in front of her and the Donnybrooke gates behind her, creaking open again.

The driver-side window opens with a screech and a smell. Lemon-lily. Sweet and sour and nauseating all at the same time. "What are you doing here? I told your mother you're not welcome here. I will not tolerate trespassing," spits Mrs. Donaldson.

Asha's head shakes *no*. Trespassing means you're on someone else's property, and Asha isn't on her property. She's on the sidewalk. If Asha could speak right now, she'd tell Mrs. Donaldson that. That she hasn't done anything wrong. That Sam was yelling. That she came to check on him. And it's not fair to get so mad at her when all she was doing was trying to help a friend. She'd never hurt Donnybrooke or Prestyn or Mrs. Donaldson, and it's not right the way they treat her just because she loves their house and sometimes acts different. She's only ever tried to be nice, and now Mrs. Donaldson is baring her white, white teeth and screaming about trespassing, and Asha has to laugh to let some of the stress escape.

"You think this is funny?" snarls Mrs. Donaldson.

At that, Asha starts running because this whole situation is the opposite of funny, and no matter what she says or does, Mrs. Donaldson hates her.

Asha reaches for her front door, but her mom opens it before Asha can.

"Asha," she says in the voice she uses when she's just pretending to be calm. She's holding her phone in her hand. "Brooke Donaldson called. She says you were there."

All the rest of the stress laughter inside Asha bursts out. It's so unfair. She loved that house before it had a roof to cover it and gates to keep people out, before Prestyn even set foot inside it, before it was even called Donnybrooke. And yet now she can't go near it without it being a complete disaster. She's not sure how long has passed, but when she doesn't have the energy to laugh anymore, her mom says, "I'm not mad, but I need to know if you were at her house."

Asha doesn't really believe that her mom isn't mad. "Not at her house. On the street near her house."

Asha's mom mutters something under her breath. Asha thinks she catches a curse word.

"Don't say that."

"I'm sorry, I just don't like her. And it's good you weren't at her house. But you were supposed to be putting up lights. I need to know that you're not going to run off to Donnybrooke. We've talked about this." Her mom closes her eyes and exhales.

"I was only gone for five minutes. And I didn't go for the house. I went for Sam."

Her mom's eyes fly open. "Sam Moss?"

"He was calling. From Donnybrooke."

"Wait a minute. Sam was there and he called you?" Confusion has replaced all the mad in her mom's voice.

Asha nods.

"He went there after soccer? With Prestyn?"

Asha flops on the couch. Her throat is tight, and she doesn't want to talk anymore.

Her mom sits down next to her. "Oh, Asha, I'm sorry. I know you miss him. I wish the situation were different. You deserve so much better. But your safety comes first. And that means not going to the Donaldsons' house, no matter what. Or anywhere near the Donaldsons' house. I hate to say it, but it really is better if you don't even think about it. Got it, sweetie?"

Asha nods and curls up tight. She got it before and she's got it now. And it turns out going was a big mistake. But she didn't know Mrs. Donaldson would catch her when Sam was yelling. She just knew he needed help.

"Sam was cold," she says.

Her mom opens her mouth like she's about to ask another question, but then she stops herself. "Just stay safe, OK?" She gives Asha a quick kiss on the forehead.

Asha knows her mom doesn't really understand. But Asha couldn't explain it to her even if she wanted to, because how do you explain something that makes no sense?

Sam

Sam has decided not to talk to Prestyn. Or Tessa. She was there, too.

Because between yesterday and today, he has run the hide-and-seek game over and over again in his head. And every time, what Prestyn said doesn't add up. He wants it to. It would be so much easier if it did. But it doesn't.

So Sam spends all of Friday ignoring her. It's the hardest he's ever worked at school, but it's worth it. He had no idea that ignoring someone could make you feel so in control. When he gets off the bus that afternoon, he takes the long way home, running the whole way. He doesn't even mind the weight of his backpack. When he gets home, his mom takes one look at him and says, "What happened at school today?"

He ignores her, too.

Sam has the same plan for Monday. Ignore Prestyn. On purpose. It's not any easier than it was on Friday, and the image of that awful weather vane above him and the dizzying view below keep popping into his mind. His head hurts by the end of the day. But the facts are the facts. He walks into school Tuesday, ready to do it all over again.

"Hey, are you trying to ignore me?" Prestyn has appeared out of nowhere and is walking next to him. "I mean you're always pretty quiet, but this seems different."

Sam gets that twitchy feeling in his legs.

"Omigod, are you mad at me about the elevator? Because it's totally not my fault that it broke."

"But you—" He catches himself. He doesn't want to yell, especially not in school.

"What? What about me? Other than it's totally unfair that you're blaming me."

Sam stops for a second and shuts his eyes. It's hard not to talk back to Prestyn. When he opens his eyes, Tessa is there, too.

"Fine, be like that," says Prestyn. "I've had you over like ten times in a row, but be mad at me for nothing."

"Five," says Sam. She's had him over five times, not ten, and three of those times he was working on the Medieval Life project by himself.

"I mean, how was I supposed to even know there was a problem? It's not like I'm psychic."

Prestyn may have a point about the elevator breaking. But how could she not know he was in trouble? That's what keeps bugging Sam.

"I called for you really loud," he blurts out. There. He told her.

"It couldn't have been that loud because no one heard you."

"That's not true. Someone heard me from further away than your house. So you have to have, too."

Prestyn bites her lip for a second. "We had the music on really loud, right, Tessa? That must be why we didn't hear."

Tessa nods at Sam, and he forces himself to look her right in the eye.

"But then you were outside. You went home when I was stuck. You had to have heard me when you left."

Tessa makes a weird noise. "I—I—I didn't," she says, and hurries off down the hall.

"Now you made her feel bad," says Prestyn, and she rushes off after her.

Now somehow it's like he's the one at fault. How did that happen?

After that, Sam goes back to his original plan. Ignore on purpose. Pretend you're an outer planet. Cold and quiet. Sam says zero words to zero kids, and they say nothing back. Meanwhile, Prestyn has returned to her usual galaxy with Tessa, the Olivias, and all those other girls who hang out with the four-letter boys.

On Thursday, Sam walks out of the cafeteria at the same time as Prestyn and Alec. They're just inches away from him, holding hands and laughing. He doesn't talk to them and they don't talk to him. It's hard to say who is ignoring who.

But Sam has an even bigger problem. Like what to do after school. He can't go home, no matter how much he wants to, because then his mom would want to know why he wasn't at soccer. He wishes he could go to the planetarium instead, to watch the stars and think about distances and masses that are enormous but quantifiable. It's the one place where he wouldn't have to ignore anyone, and no one would ignore him. They might even think he was smart. It's probably the closest he could get to feeling like he's not at school while still on the Castleton grounds. But Sam doesn't think he is allowed there now.

He stands out front and watches the eighth graders take down the flags. They're shaking out the Castleton one, with its three twisted snakes. Their forked red tongues seem to wiggle. Why on earth did the school decide to use snakes when they could have put a planetarium on their flag instead? What a mistake.

As all the kids head in tight groups to their buses, Sam wonders if Castleton made other mistakes, too. Like picking him.

"Sam!" Prestyn has appeared next to him again. How does she do that?

"I want to tell you that I don't think you should come over

after school today. Not if you're going to blame me for something I didn't do."

"OK," says Sam. He wasn't expecting to go anyway.

"That's what I mean. How can I be friends with you when you're still mad at me?"

Now that's a really weird thing for Prestyn to say. Like they were actually friends in the first place. They weren't, were they? She never hung out with him the way she hangs out with the kids she eats lunch with, and she barely talks to him at school. She doesn't even talk to him that much when he's at her house.

He turns toward her, but she's already stepping on the bus that will take her home to Donnybrooke.

The "in session" light outside the planetarium door is off. Sam exhales. He's not too late for Astronomy Club. Technically the club is for high school students, which is why he's never tried to go before. But this afternoon he started thinking about it, and the more he does, the more he realizes that rule doesn't really make sense for him. It might not even be an actual rule. More of a custom. He pulls open the door.

As he steps inside, a large, kind woman says, "Hello, Sam! May I help you?" It's Ms. Alexander, the high school astronomy and physics teacher. The day Sam visited, he had a whole long conversation with her about the size of the visible universe.

"I want to go to Astronomy Club today."

"Oh, dear . . . we'd love to have you, but the club is only for high school students."

"I know that," says Sam. "But I bet I know as much as any of those kids about space."

Ms. Alexander laughs a little, which is a bad sign since what Sam said wasn't funny. "Oh, Sam, I'll bet you do. And I wish the rules were different because I'm sure you'd make some great contributions."

"Then why—"

"I'm so sorry, Sam, but the rules are the rules. But hey, who's your science teacher?"

That is a really, truly, exceptionally stupid rule. Black-hole-magnitude stupid. It should get sucked up and disappear forever.

"Sam?"

"It's Ms. Springer."

Ms. Alexander checks a board on the wall. "Your class is scheduled for tomorrow. So you'll be back real soon."

She shuts the planetarium door. The sign outside lights up red with a message that seems aimed right at Sam: *In Session. Closed. Do Not Enter.*

Sam doesn't notice Dr. Deutsch's footsteps until it's too late. He's sitting by his locker, wishing this Househaunt basement were really a Spacehaunt pulsar, when he hears them and then a fake, singsongy voice: "Samuel Moss. All Castleton students who stay after school must be in a designated activity."

Under the hall lights, Dr. Deutsch's blocky black shoes shine like the Witch-Ones he's about to suck up with his vacuum. There. *Bzzzzp.* He's got them.

"Excuse me, Sam? Where are you supposed to be right now?"

Sam pauses the game. Even with it off, he can't think of an answer.

"If you're just sitting here, you'll need to call your mom to have her pick you up. Or I could call her for you."

"No! She can't come. Not now." Sam doesn't want to think about what she would say if she got a call, especially from Dr. Deutsch. Once she learned he didn't go to soccer today, she would ask about what he did all of the other Thursdays, and when she found out the truth, she would be so mad. And she would know just how far he really is from being Castleton material.

"Hmmm. Well, I suppose you could go to chess in Room 112. Don't kids like you love chess?"

It's such a strange question said in such a strange way that Sam looks right up at her. He's never even played chess. "What do you mean?"

"Oh, just guessing it would be something you'd like." She has the same crocodile smile she had on the first day of school when she put up the "Miracle Boy" slide that caused all the trouble, and Sam realizes she's saying something about him being different. About him being autistic. One of the hall lights buzzes and blinks, and he looks away. If he could have just stayed in the planetarium, everything would be fine right now.

"Why is Astronomy Club only for high school students?" he says. "That rule makes absolutely no sense. There are kids in middle school who know way more about outer space than most high school students. Way more."

Like Ms. Alexander, Dr. Deutsch laughs, but hers is short and mean, not soft and kind. "I'll take that under advisement. In the meantime, however, since neither that nor sitting in the hall playing video games is an option, let's try Chess Club. Unless you'd like me to call your mom for you."

The first thing the chess instructor, Mr. Hockley, says when he learns Sam doesn't know how to play is, "How can a kid get to the seventh grade and not know the difference between a bishop and a rook?" After he shows Sam the basic moves, he asks if anyone will partner up with Sam. No one volunteers. Mr. Hockley seems to think that this is because Sam doesn't know how to play, and Sam doesn't bother explaining that no one wants to partner with him in science or any other class anymore, no matter how good he is at it. Instead he sits up front with Mr. Hockley, who spends the next forty minutes loudly droning on about opening moves. By the end of the activity period, Sam can't help but wonder if soccer with the four-letter boys would be better than this.

The next day, in the echo chamber of the planetarium, he gets his answer. A targeted two-word answer.

"Miracle Boy."

Asha

Asha knows she should be happy that Joanna is over, but the truth is it's kind of stressful on a day like today. It's too damp to climb trees, and Asha's house is all out of Joanna's favorite snack and her favorite drink—double chocolate chip cookies and black-cherry-flavored seltzer. There's not much to do but stare out the window, watch the drizzle come and go, and wait for Joanna to tell her she's bored. And to see if Sam is going home with Prestyn. It is Thursday after all.

"Are you looking for Sam?" asks Joanna.

"How did you know?" Asha doesn't take her eyes off the line of kids walking up Maplevale Lane. It's a little hard to tell who everyone is with their windbreakers, but this batch looks too short.

"Doesn't he go home with them?" says Joanna, pointing to two kids lagging behind the rest. Asha hadn't even noticed them.

But they are Prestyn and Tessa. And Sam is not with them. Not behind them, not in front of them. Asha wonders if Sam is actually at soccer. If Sam were here—the old Sam—she wouldn't be worried about the drizzle or him being happy. They'd already be playing Househaunt.

"What do you want to do?" asks Joanna. It's her polite way of saying she's bored, Asha knows.

"Play Househaunt." That really is the only thing Asha can think of.

Joanna pushes her bangs out of her face. "OK, I guess. Just don't laugh at me if I die right away."

"Of course I wouldn't," says Asha.

"No, you wouldn't," agrees Joanna. "Also, I might get freaked out by the monsters. They're not too gross, are they?"

"They're mostly silly. Though they can pop up out of nowhere."

Asha plops on the couch and Joanna sits next to her, just like Rohan and his friends do when they play on their phones together. She wishes he were here right now to teach Joanna the way he taught Sam and her all those years ago. But he's not, and Sam's not, so it's up to Asha. She cracks the window for some air and opens Househaunt. Her biggest, fanciest house comes up. It hasn't been cleaned in months, and it's trembling like there's an idling motor under it. A sure sign of a monster infestation. Ugh.

"You copied that mean girl's house?"

Asha follows Joanna's gaze out the back window to Donny-brooke. It's magical in the mist and feels close enough to touch. Asha wishes she were there so badly her chest aches. For a second, she wonders if it would wish for her, too, if it could.

"They look the same," says Joanna.

"No, they don't," says Asha. "This house has no weather vane, only two turrets—both identical—and the spiral stairs are in the front, not back. And inside, there's no elevator, and my kitchen doesn't have a big island in the middle, and my basement is just one big, open room, but in Donnybrooke there's a wine cellar and a utility room and a gym and more. The only thing I have that is the same is the ceiling in the bedroom with the turret, and my bed isn't circle-shaped. So it's really only the ceiling. That's it. Seriously."

Asha can feel Joanna staring at her. But it's true that her House-haunt house really isn't like Donnybrooke, and not just because it doesn't have a lucky girl living in it.

"You've been inside it?" says Joanna.

At first, Asha thinks Joanna is talking about her Househaunt house, which isn't even real, but then she understands. "Twice," she says softly.

"Did you used to be friends with the mean girl?"

"Yes. No. My first time—" How can she explain all the memories in her head? The moment she thought Prestyn was her friend, and the moment she realized how wrong she was. The shrieks of the girls, the slam of the door. The soft carpet littered with princess dresses. The fish on the weather vane, desperate to escape. A flash of liquid, like sunlight you could touch.

And then her mom's hand cold on her wrist, pulling her toward the door.

Asha still isn't sure what she did wrong. Her mom has always said that Asha didn't do anything, but of course she did, and it must have been big. Otherwise she'd have been invited back like all of the other girls.

"What happened?"

Asha tells her the truth. "I don't know."

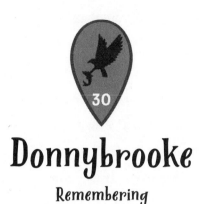

Donnybrooke

Remembering

Donnybrooke knows. How can it not remember its very first party, the very first time it was shown off to Coreville?

Everything was so pristine then. So perfect. Not a hint of the broken stairs or Cheeto-filled vents, the family arguments or stony silences to come. Donnybrooke was new enough that little Prestyn would still get lost from time to time. "It's so big!" she'd say once she'd found her way back to her parents.

"It's our dream house," Mrs. Donaldson would explain. "And the bigger the house, the bigger the dreams."

"And you need the biggest dreams to be the best," Mr. Donaldson would add.

And Donnybrooke understood. *It* was what made the Donaldsons the best. Without it, they might just be ordinary. Three ordinary people living ordinary lives with ordinary

problems. Then again, without the Donaldsons, Donnybrooke wouldn't even exist. But together, with their beauty and their stature, the four of them could rise above the rest of Coreville. And their first party would be their chance to prove it.

Mrs. Donaldson planned every last detail of the party, a mother-daughter event. Indeed, she'd been working on the guest list longer than the construction crew had been working on Donnybrooke. She invited all the right people—Dahlia George, who wrote for *Mansion Magnificence* magazine (how better to get a feature on Donnybrooke?), Bree Kelso, who lived in a restored Victorian on the edge of town that just happened to be the second largest in Coreville (and had already been written up in *Mansion Magnificence*), and a slew of Castleton moms with girls around Prestyn's age. Mrs. Donaldson also invited the neighbors, even though they lived in modest homes that could fit inside Donnybrooke's basement with room to spare. Mr. Donaldson had encouraged her to "make peace" since a few of the more unreasonable neighbors were upset about all the trees that had been cleared when the mansion was built.

"I didn't build the biggest house on the top of town so I could 'make peace' with people I don't care about. I built it so I wouldn't have to," said Mrs. Donaldson.

"Don't worry. You can still invite everyone worth knowing," said Mr. Donaldson.

"You better believe I can. That's why I'm paying Coreville Farmcart catering prices," said Mrs. Donaldson, and they both laughed.

Oh, don't judge them. They used to joke like that, those two. At least they were laughing then. Besides, who doesn't want to know who to know when they settle somewhere new?

Still, jokes aside, this party mattered. This was the party that would set the tone for their lives in Coreville, that would determine all the parties that followed, the ones the Donaldsons hosted and the ones they'd be invited to. In other words, this party in this house was what was going to make people want to be with them.

Asha and her mother are the first to arrive. As they enter, Asha's eyes widen and her mouth drops open. Donnybrooke was built to be admired, and right then and there, it knows it will fulfill its destiny.

Asha's mother hands Mrs. Donaldson a small gift bag, and they exchange pleasantries. Prestyn politely introduces herself, just as she practiced, while Asha runs her fingers along the foyer walls, which are painted to look like marble, and cranes her neck for a better view of the crystal chandelier. She's so taken by Donnybrooke's magnificence, she doesn't even hear Mrs. Donaldson ask for her name the first few times.

Mrs. Donaldson pointedly repeats herself. "And what's *your* name?" Asha's mother nudges her.

"Hi!" says Asha. Mrs. Donaldson looks taken aback. The girl's voice apparently has a bit more enthusiasm than Mrs. Donaldson was expecting.

"This is Asha," says her mom as Asha runs off into the main section of the house. She clutches the hem of her dress and twirls through several rooms before her mom collects her and returns her to the foyer, breathless.

"There's an atrium, and archways, and a spiral staircase and a regular staircase, and Ionic columns and Corinthian columns, and oval, circle, square, and rectangle windows. All in one house!" announces Asha.

"Wow! That is quite a list," says Dahlia George of *Mansion Magnificence*, who has just arrived. She lets out a small laugh. It could almost be mistaken for a snicker.

"I have never, ever seen a house like this before!" Asha continues.

"Nor have I," murmurs Dahlia George. Mrs. Donaldson's cheeks flush to match the bright pink of the flowers on her blouse. She sucks in her cheeks and excuses herself for a moment, leaving everyone to socialize in the foyer.

"Can I go up and see your room?" Asha says to Prestyn.

"Sure," replies Prestyn with a shrug.

When Mrs. Donaldson returns with a mostly drained glass of wine, both of the girls are already upstairs. Both of their mothers frown at the empty staircase.

Asha explores the second-floor hallway while Prestyn trails behind. Asha knocks on each elegant column, stands in the arched window that is taller than she is, peeks in the various rooms, each with a different layout than the one before. She gasps and giggles with each delightful discovery, and Donnybrooke feels any lingering tension from the foyer dissolve. When she gets to Prestyn's room, she squeals out loud. Then she runs to the plush pink rug in the middle of the room and flops down on her back like she is about to make a snow angel. For a moment, Prestyn stands in the doorway, her brow furrowed, just watching. But then she joins Asha on the rug. Both girls' fingers sink in so deeply that it looks like pink grass is sprouting between them. Only a blade separates their pinkies.

"Wow!" says Asha.

"Yeah!" says Prestyn.

Both girls start giggling. Prestyn turns to look at Asha, but Asha's eyes are set on the ceiling.

It is no ordinary ceiling, but the inside of a turret, the roundness dissolving to a point. It is so high that the cleaning crew that comes each Friday has to use a real ladder—not

a stepladder—to clean the cobwebs. Donnybrooke knew it was an unusual ceiling, but until now it did not know it was so beautiful. Precious. Something to behold. No one—not darling Prestyn, who sleeps under it every night; not Mrs. Donaldson, who helped to design it—no one has looked at it the way Asha does, like it's one of the wonders of the world. It is a revelation to Donnybrooke. And perhaps to Prestyn, too?

"I want to live here," says Asha.

"You could come back. Maybe for a sleepover," says Prestyn.

"Sleepover?" says Asha.

"Have you been on a sleepover? I have twice. I think I'm going to have a sleepover birthday."

"Prestyn! What are you doing?" says Mrs. Donaldson. She's standing in the open doorway.

Prestyn, startled, sits straight up. Asha, however, doesn't even blink away from the ceiling.

"Prestyn, please come here now," Mrs. Donaldson says. Prestyn has heard that tone before. She's there in a flash. Mrs. Donaldson lowers her voice. "Haven't you noticed that Asha is . . . a little different?"

Prestyn nods, her wide eyes on her mother.

"And I think you know better than to lie down in the middle of a party."

Prestyn stares down at the floor. She doesn't reply.

Mrs. Donaldson takes a deep breath. She kneels down and presses her forehead to her daughter's. "Listen to me, honey, this is important. I know what it's like to feel so lonely and left out, you just want to cry. I never, ever want you to have to feel that way. Here's the thing: having the right friends will go a long way to making sure you don't." She picks a piece of pink fluff off Prestyn's dress. "I just want you to be happy."

"I was happy on the floor with her." Prestyn pouts.

"Oh, Pressie, please don't be difficult. I'm trying so hard to do what's best for all of us. Can you trust me that this will all make sense one day?"

Prestyn nods, and Mrs. Donaldson kisses the top of her head. The doorbell rings, and they snap to attention. "Now let's try to put on a smile and our very best manners," says Mrs. Donaldson. "A whole bunch of *other* girls are coming. Girls more like you."

Indeed there are. A troop of them arrive en masse with their mothers. Prestyn stands by Mrs. Donaldson, and together they appraise each of their guests. Soon Prestyn is leading Addison, Tessa, a couple of Olivias, and a set of twins, Emma and Ava, up the stairs like the princess she is meant to be.

Unlike Asha, none of these girls stop along the way, yet by the time they reach Prestyn's room, they've already fallen

under her spell. When Prestyn says, "It's time for dolls," they all want dolls. When Prestyn announces, "Dolls are boring," they all drop theirs like last week's trash. When Prestyn declares she will dress up like Elsa, they all clamor to be Elsa, too. A melee erupts in the closet. There are only two Elsa dresses, and no one wants to be Belle, Tiana, Snow White, Cinderella, or even Anna when Prestyn is being Elsa.

Asha is still on the plush rug, wisely plugging her ears as the other girls squeak and squawk about. She doesn't move until Prestyn, leading the march out of the closet, stumbles over her foot. The extra Elsa costume flies out of her hand, and the other girls fall on it like it's a loose football.

"Why are you still on my rug? It's not good manners," says Prestyn.

"When can we have a sleepover?" says Asha.

A few of the other girls giggle.

"You're not supposed to lie down during a party," says Prestyn.

Asha closes her fist around clumps of pink carpet and laughs, though the sound isn't a happy one. Meanwhile, Prestyn marches back to the girls and reclaims the extra Elsa dress. A bidding war ensues, with Addison and the bigger Olivia in tight competition for the lead. Olivia promises Prestyn a pink-frosted cupcake cake, while Addison offers up tube after tube of smelly, sticky lip gloss. Then, out of nowhere, little Tessa Ferrer says, "I can braid your hair just like Elsa's."

"You can?" says Prestyn, turning away from the other children and, more importantly, the dreadful lip gloss. "You know how to braid hair?"

Tessa nods shyly.

"OK," says Prestyn. She sweeps her hair over her left shoulder. Tessa reaches for the dress, but Prestyn holds it tight. "Braid my hair first."

Tessa eyes the dark cascade. Her own hair, pale blond and wispy, is barely to her chin and thin enough to show her scalp in a strong wind. Tessa divides Prestyn's hair in three uneven pieces, two of which are too thick to fit in Tessa's small hands. Tessa tries again and again, while the other girls make their picks from the remaining princess dresses.

"I can do it!" says Asha, jumping up. It's quite a surprise to Donnybrooke, which has been quite enjoying her undivided admiration.

"You can braid hair?" asks Tessa, dropping Prestyn's mane.

Asha shakes out her own thick, dark hair, breaks it into three pieces, and does a few neat twists.

"I can do it," she says, and Tessa steps aside, seemingly happy to pass her job on.

"You can't," says Prestyn.

"I can," says Asha. She takes a handful of her hair and a handful of Prestyn's. "It's the same."

"It's not," says Prestyn, pulling away. "Nothing about us is the same. Not our hair, not our skin, not our eyes. We're different."

"I like Elsa," says Asha.

"I hate Elsa," says Prestyn. "*Frozen* is stupid."

It's such a strange thing for Prestyn to say because it's simply not true. She loves *Frozen*. Her bed has not one but two Elsa throw pillows. And the girls' hair *is* very similar. In fact, the whole situation is so strange; it's like nothing Donnybrooke has experienced to date. Asha is reacting precisely as a guest should to the splendor of Donnybrooke. Isn't this what the Donaldsons want? And yet Prestyn isn't looking back. She flounces out of her room with a line of girls behind her. Addison, bringing up the rear, yells, "Don't follow us," and slams the door so hard the walls shake.

But just as things quiet down in Prestyn's room, they heat up downstairs. Now, before you read this part, please remember how nervous Mrs. Donaldson was, how much this party meant to her—indeed, she said she hadn't been this stressed since her wedding day. Again, it was her first party in a new home in a new town. And it's not like she could figure out who to be friends with based on who had a similarly impressive home because no one else did. She was under a lot of pressure, and anyone can make a mistake under those circumstances.

Right away, from their dress and their manners, it's clear that Mrs. Donaldson has invited some excellent prospects. They converse effortlessly; they dress elegantly; the best among them compliment Donnybrooke's stature and features. Only one woman stands apart. Asha's mother. She keeps checking her watch and glancing up at the ceiling as if she could see through it to check on her daughter. She can't, of course. Donnybrooke is sufficiently well constructed to be opaque. She makes a bit of small talk and nibbles on a tea sandwich. Then she steps away to get herself half a glass of white wine.

She returns to a lively conversation about private school admissions. Mrs. Donaldson has been dying for Prestyn to get into Castleton, but they're still waiting to hear. Many of the mothers here have children who already attend, and that must only add to Mrs. Donaldson's stress. She drains her wineglass and says to Asha's mom, "You're so lucky you don't have to worry about any of this."

"Pardon me?" Asha's mom's fingers tighten on the stem of her crystal glass.

"This is just not something you'll ever have to deal with for Asha."

"I—I suppose not." The glass in her hand trembles. Her gaze falters.

The conversation around them stops. A few of the ladies stare at the ground, perhaps admiring the lovely dappling on the cowhide rug.

"She's very . . . uh . . . unique, isn't she?"

Asha's mom straightens. Her mouth opens and shuts, and when her words finally come, they are surprisingly soft. "I don't know. There are other kids in town who . . ." She trails off midsentence, inhales sharply, and stares hard at a point on the atrium ceiling. Then she abruptly turns to leave.

But before she can, Mrs. Donaldson, always quick with her words, says, "Here in town, huh? Think it's something in the water?" She smiles halfway and gets that look in her eye, the one that means she's sure she's won. "Maybe I should stick with the wine." She tosses her head back in a throaty laugh. She can't see the stunned faces of the other guests, the time slowing as Asha's mom spins around, glass in hand.

"Maybe you should," says Asha's mom as all the wine in her glass flies out. For just that instant, it separates and the sun shines through the drops of gold. Liquid made light. Then it streams back into liquid that lands squarely on the still-laughing Mrs. Donaldson.

Asha's mom stares at her hand like it's turned into a snake.

The entire room, right down to the climate control, is completely silent.

Then fast footsteps come down the stairs, and Asha's voice: "There's a fish up there. It's going to get eaten."

That breaks the spell. A few women—some of the best dressed of the lot, in fact—pat Mrs. Donaldson down with napkins. Thankfully the shock on their faces while she was talking has been replaced with sympathy now that she is dripping wet. But the others, including Dahlia George, the *Mansion Magnificence* writer, and Bree Kelso, who lives in that old house that's almost as big as Donnybrooke, are already edging toward the exit.

"The fish," Asha starts again. "The fish up there—"

"We have to go. Now," says Asha's mother, grabbing her hand and talking over her.

As her mother leads her toward the door, Asha's eyes reach for Donnybrooke's finest details: the atrium window, the spiral staircase, the arched entryway. Whatever nervousness she had about the mighty weather vane seems to slip away. Her last look is as awestruck as her first.

"When can I come back for a sleepover?" she says before she leaves the gates.

The party breaks up soon after, the guests scattering back to their homes. Though the ending is a touch awkward, on

the whole, the party can only be considered a success. While it's true Donnybrooke was never featured in *Mansion Magnificence*, and that the Donaldsons have never received an invitation to the Kelsos' annual New Year's Eve bash, overall, the party led them to just the lives they wanted. Within weeks, Mrs. Donaldson had made enough friends to fill her calendar and then some. Mr. Donaldson found the professional success he craved, and indeed some of the party guests signed contracts with him that very month. Prestyn became the princess of Castleton Academy. And Donnybrooke became the most sought-after site for Coreville's finest social events.

Yet Mrs. Donaldson is stuck, still harboring her curious grudge against Asha, and now Prestyn seems to be following suit. If it were up to Donnybrooke, the Donaldsons would appreciate the girl for her exquisite taste in homes. But years on, there's still no sign of that happening.

And so Donnybrooke's biggest admirer admires it from afar.

Asha

"I don't know," Asha says again to Joanna. "But I always remember how beautiful it was inside."

"Beautiful?" Joanna wrinkles her nose. "But it's so strange-looking."

It's one thing when Asha's mom insults Donnybrooke, or even Rohan, but Joanna? How can she, of all people, say this? "You draw it. A lot."

"I draw it because I don't understand it. All those mismatched pieces—it's like chunks of houses squashed together. There's no . . . harmony. Why would you build a house so fancy but so . . . ugly?"

"Ugly?" Asha stares down at her phone. She tries to focus on the shaking turrets. She doesn't want to act as upset as she feels.

"Your house is nicer than that one," says Joanna, pointing at Asha's phone. "And your real house, too. A lot nicer."

"No, they're not." How can Joanna be so wrong? Asha's real house is completely boring right down to its front door, and the only reason her Househaunt house doesn't look more like Donnybrooke is because the game doesn't allow you to put all of Donnybrooke's cool features in one house. It's not Donnybrooke's fault that it's like an oversized box of chocolates with so many wonderful things inside. So what if it's not like all the other houses out there? It's the luckiest house there is. "Donnybrooke has all these different columns on every floor—"

"But why would a house like that even need columns? And if it's going to have them, shouldn't they all be the same? It's like with the windows. Whoever built that house was completely confused."

"But all those windows let in so much light. And the columns cast the coolest shadows. It all makes it so lovely like, like . . ." Asha trails off as her throat tightens. She blinks hard. It's clear Joanna doesn't understand. No one ever does.

As Asha's eyes open, the left turret of her Househaunt house explodes. Asha and Joanna both yelp.

A swarm of Zombie-Selves emerge in party mode with balloons and blowers and one very large brain. A pack of At-ticks follow close at their heels. The Zombies try to move the brain out of reach, but instead they drop it, and it slides down the main roof and is caught by a swarm of Bed-Thugs, which take little nips at it. The At-ticks catch up and start crawling in its folds while the Zombies grab at the bug-free pieces.

"That's so gross!" squeals Joanna. "You told me this game wasn't gross!"

"I didn't know!" says Asha, fumbling to close the app while a Zombie slurps up a bloody, bumpy bit of brain. She has never seen anything like it. Her house has never been so infested before. Rohan had warned her it could get icky, but either he or Sam always cleaned out the monsters before they got to this point. Sam loved doing that. Even if he didn't want to be her friend anymore, he could still just have helped with her house. But he didn't, and now everything is getting messed up with Joanna, who is taking out her sketchbook because she hates Househaunt. Asha thinks she might hate it, too, now.

The first thing Asha does when Joanna leaves is text Rohan about what happened because Sam hasn't been killing her monsters. He replies right away.

Oh, yeah, Brain Party. It's pretty sick.

Only happens when the toughest houses haven't been maintained.

But don't worry about it. You can put your house in vacation mode for a week and the monsters will stop multiplying.

I'll get 'em all when I come home for Thanksgiving. That way your house won't be condemned.

We'll get it back to being Asha-perfect.

Those are all good answers to the questions she asked, really good actually, and without any of his silly college talk.

But they don't help at all with the question she was trying to ask: How come when one part of a friendship ends, all of them have to?

Sam

"Miracle Boy."

"Miracle Boy."

"Miracle Boy."

It's everywhere. Cafeteria, classrooms, bus, and all the places in between. Somehow, though, he hates it the most when he's in the planetarium. That was supposed to be the one place that made Castleton special. That made it just right for him.

But now it's the opposite. Even when he talks, which is not often, no one responds. It's like Castleton has turned into outer space and his sound waves can't travel. They just stay lodged in his mouth. Most of the time, light waves don't seem to bounce off of him either. That's the only upside to being called Miracle Boy. It's proof he exists.

He doesn't want to talk about it. Not to anyone, not even his mom. Especially not his mom. All she says is, "You're not the first middle schooler to ignore your mom. The way you're acting is perfectly normal."

Normal. That's what she wants, isn't it? But then she shouldn't have talked to that annoying reporter. If that stupid article hadn't been written, Dr. Deutsch wouldn't have had the chance to blab to the whole school about it, and no one would call him by his stupid nickname. He wouldn't be dreading the bus, the cafeteria, even the planetarium.

But nothing about this situation is normal. Nothing about this situation is good.

Thursdays are the worst because then he has to stay late after school, and he always gets stuck playing with Mr. Hockley, whose voice has only gotten louder. He talks to Sam like he's dense for still not having mastered the rules of chess, as if Sam has any interest in learning them. The heater on the late bus is broken, so it's colder than the Donnybrooke wine cellar. The wine cellar wasn't actually that cold. It would have been OK with a jacket. Sam zips his up and wonders what might be happening there today.

The next Thursday—actually Wednesday night—he makes a decision. He won't go to school. He just won't go.

"I don't feel well," he says when his mom comes in to wake

him up the next morning. "My stomach hurts. My head hurts, too." It's true, they do. They have for days.

His mom leans over and presses her hand to his forehead. She's warmer than he is.

"You don't feel like you have a fever." To his surprise, she sits at the foot of the bed. "But I think I might know the real reason you don't want to go to school."

Sam's stomach flip-flops for real. He's pretty sure she doesn't, and he can't tell her. He just can't. But as he sinks deeper in his bed, he feels a little lighter now that at least someone has finally noticed that everything isn't perfect. Maybe if he lies very still, she'll do all the talking and decide that he needs to stay home.

"I know we've been so excited about how going to Castleton is such a great opportunity. But along the way, maybe we forgot what a huge transition this is." Her words are coming faster, which always gets Sam a little nervous. "Switching schools would be hard for any kid, and middle school is hard for any kid, and you're doing both at the same time. Of course it's overwhelming sometimes. It would be for anyone."

She pauses. Sam wonders if this is a long way of telling him she thinks he's not Castleton material after all. But her voice isn't at all sad or disappointed, and he's sure it would be if that's what she were trying to say.

His mom lets out a long, slow sigh. "So your dad and I have

been talking, and I think he'll be OK with me telling you already that we think we've come up with a solution just for you."

Solution? Sam is listening hard because he sure as heck doesn't have any answers.

"We want to give you a little reward for how hard you're working. Well, actually a big reward."

Not having to go to school today is the biggest reward Sam can think of at the moment.

"What would you think of a trip to the Kennedy Space Center and Cape Canaveral?"

Sam sits straight up. "In Florida?"

"That's the only one I know of." His mom is grinning ear-to-ear.

What would he think of a trip to see the *Atlantis* space shuttle and the Saturn V and all the most important rockets? The place where basically every major launch has occurred in the United States? He would love it, of course. But what on earth does that have to do with what his mom was just saying? He thought they were talking about school.

"Sam?"

"I—I—yes!" says Sam.

"Then, if you can just keep doing what you're doing at school, Dad and I will take you over spring break as a reward."

"Spring break?" That's like a time galaxy away. He's not sure he can even keep doing what he's doing at school until the end of today.

"You've got this, Sammy. I know you do."

He shakes off his covers and climbs out of bed. His mom gives his hand a quick squeeze.

"We really are so proud of you. And you can always text me this afternoon if you're not feeling well enough for soccer," she says. "But hopefully this talk will be just what you needed."

This talk plus a time machine to take him straight to spring break.

Sam makes it through the day with the usual amount of "Miracle Boy," maybe less. But what he really needs is a day with none.

"Sam?"

He jumps. Prestyn is right next to him. If it weren't impossible, he'd swear she could teleport.

"Do you want to come over today?"

"What?" He stares at her face, really stares at all the parts, but they look the same as always.

"It's Thursday."

"But . . . I . . ." Doesn't she remember the last time? And their fight? And that he hasn't been over there for four Thursdays in a row? So what if one of them was Thanksgiving? "I don't do that anymore."

She rolls her eyes, a big roll, like she always does. "Are you seriously still hung up on that stupid elevator glitch? Like it was my fault? Anyway, it's been fixed."

Sam's phone is heavy in his hands. All he has to do is text his mom: *Come get me.*

"I thought we had fun. Except for that one time, and we don't even have to play that stupid game. Otherwise I'll be all alone. No one else can come today, not even Tessa."

The message app is already open on Sam's phone, just waiting for him to type.

"I'll be so bored by myself, but whatever. If you'd rather go home or to your friend Asha's, that's your choice, I guess."

Sam's phone catches the sun, and he blinks away the glare. That's all the time it takes to decide.

Going to soccer, he texts. Then he follows Prestyn, hopping on the bus just before the doors close.

Sam remembers that time when his mom had left out the files when she was working on the application to Castleton. He flipped open a report that said, *Sam limits himself to parallel play. He plays near other children, but not with them.* Reading that made him feel squelchy inside, like the therapist was describing a Zombie-Self and not the actual kid he used to be. But here at Donny-brooke, he realizes parallel play is like ninety percent of what

Prestyn and Tessa do. They just sit next to each other and play on their phones. It's what the kids at school do most of the time, too.

And that's what he and Prestyn are doing right now. She is on her phone, scrolling through some social media app. And he is on his phone, building and rebuilding an easy-mode Househaunt house—a center-hall colonial laid out just like his real house—because it's nerve-racking enough being at Prestyn's without throwing in a bunch of murderous monsters. After his eighth time building it perfectly, he realizes he is incredibly bored.

It's the best he's felt in a long time.

As Prestyn taps away at her phone, Sam decides maybe he can handle a monster or two after all. He picks out the wrong pantry just for the fun of it. The moment he drops it in his kitchen, Prestyn rests her phone on the counter.

"Aren't you bored?" she says. She is like a mind reader sometimes. "Don't you want to do something?"

Sam rummages through his Househaunt kitchen searching for something to knock out a fresh pair of Vampire-Chefs that have now emerged.

"We could play a game," she says.

"I am playing a game." He notices a whole string of garlic bulbs hanging on the wall as decoration. That must be what he's supposed to use. He just needs to loosen a bulb.

"Very funny. We could play a real game. Like hide-and-seek."

"No!" Sam's hand slips, and he launches the entire string at the Vampire-Chef closest to him. The garlic circles the monster's neck, and it keels over. Which might make Sam happy if he weren't being threatened by another Vampire-Chef. And Prestyn, too.

"Omigod! You are still mad about the elevator even though it totally wasn't my fault. Besides, I told you we got it fixed."

Sam runs out of his Househaunt kitchen. His feet are twitching. He wants to run out of Prestyn's, too.

"Look, I'll go with you. The two of us can ride it together. As much as you want. We don't even have to play the game. We can just do elevator rides the whole time so you know it's fixed. Would that be OK?"

Sam stares at his phone even after he's shut down the game. Is he being inflexible? Maybe. She's already said he doesn't have to do any of the things he doesn't want to.

"OK." His arms get goose bumps as soon as he says that. "But I want to get my jacket first."

"Of course you can get your jacket. Why would that even be an issue?"

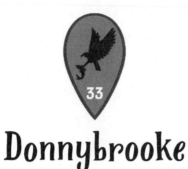

Donnybrooke

The Perpetual-Motion Machine

Children these days! They simply can't make up their minds. They're either hot or they're cold. They either can't stop eating guacamole or they can't stop smearing it on every available surface. They're either pushing Donnybrooke's elevator button to go up or they're pressing it to go down. And of all the noteworthy features in Donnybrooke's interior, the elevator is among the least interesting. The mirrored walls provide something of an infinity effect, but all that Prestyn and Sam can see are themselves. Over and over. Up and down. Cellar to roof deck. Roof deck to cellar. There are times when Donnybrooke can't help but conclude that this younger generation is a bit full of themselves.

Prestyn makes a silly face, crossing her eyes and sticking out her tongue. Her dad taught her that face one of her first

times in the elevator, and they had a good laugh over it. It's quite ridiculous. But very pleasantly so. Seeing her like this now, so silly and so friendly with the boy, can't help but soften Donnybrooke a bit. Prestyn is its princess after all. Whatever happened the last time the boy was on the roof deck must have been a misunderstanding. Just because Donnybrooke assumed the worst doesn't make it true. Of course Donny-brooke has always been lucky to have the Donaldsons, and it still is. Of course it is. See, even the boy is making a funny face now.

Prestyn taps the button again. And up they go.

This time, when they get to the roof deck, Prestyn gets off and walks to the edge, surveying the town below. She seems as happy as the very first time she saw the view and yelled, "I'm the princess of the whole town!" and her father scooped her up and said, "Of course you are, darling." It's been so long since then, but the view is the same. Better actually. This time, the leaves are gone.

"Coming?" Prestyn asks the boy. The sun is setting, and the shadows are long.

The boy stands at the threshold, murmuring something to himself. Then, in the time it takes for Prestyn to stroll along the entire perimeter of the deck, he takes two steps off. He cranes his neck, takes one more step, and looks toward the mighty eagle weather vane. His eyes grow big, just like Asha's did all those years ago. He shoves his fists in his pockets and practically leaps back to the elevator.

The boy is fast. But he needn't be. Despite its cracks, the roof deck isn't about to fail him. And neither is Prestyn. She is propping open the door, flashing him her sweetest smile. It takes him a second, but he smiles back. As the door closes, both children make silly faces in the mirror.

And down they go. Again.

But Donnybrooke won't complain. After all, even the boy appreciates it today.

Asha

Asha cannot wait for Joanna to come over today. It's the last Thursday before winter break, and Asha has the perfect surprise for her: architectural drafting paper. The sheets are as big as the surface of Asha's desk and covered in perfect squares so you can get the proportions just right. It's sort of a present for Asha, too, because now she won't have to worry about whether the weather is good for climbing trees or whether her house might explode into a Brain Party just as she's trying to teach Househaunt to Joanna. Not that Asha is planning to do *that* ever again. Sure, Joanna *says* she's not upset anymore, but Asha doesn't believe it. Joanna is always nice. But the drafting paper, now that's something that will actually make Joanna happy.

"I have a surprise for you," Asha says to Joanna as soon as she comes to the cafeteria.

Joanna drops her binder and smiles. Her light-blue sweatshirt is almost the exact color of the lines on the drafting paper. "A surprise? What is it?"

"I can't tell or it won't be a surprise. You'll find out after school when you come over."

"Today?" says Lexi from the other side of Joanna.

"Not today," says Joanna, shaking her head.

"It's Thursday," says Asha. She's sure it is. She had her science test, scheduled for Thursday morning, today. And yesterday, on Wednesday, she had an appointment with her psychologist, Dr. Wells, where she came up with strategies to manage things that might make her anxious, like, for example, Joanna coming over after everything went so wrong last time.

"We're going to the volleyball meeting today," says Lexi. "Actually every Thursday for the next three months. There's a clinic starting in January."

Since when have Lexi and Joanna started doing things together? And since when have they played volleyball? "You do ballet with Sloane."

"I used to do ballet with Sloane. I quit," says Lexi. "I didn't love it."

"Did Sloane quit, too?"

"Nope," says Lexi.

"But you and Sloane always do everything together," says

Asha. It's true, they do. Or at least they did. Asha used to dream about having a friendship just like Lexi and Sloane's—where your friend liked the things you liked, and never got bored with you or mad at you, and invited you for sleepovers every weekend, maybe even twice a weekend, and loved all the things that were weird about you. How can Lexi leave that all behind just because she doesn't love ballet?

Lexi bites her lip and says slowly, "I think Sloane and Connor are doing everything together now." She points to the popular-kid table, where Sloane is sitting next to Connor, who is in the middle of his cupcake trick again. He gulps it down whole, and Sloane cheers as he licks the icing off his fingers. Then she takes his hand and waves it in the air like he's won a medal or something. It's so . . . unexpected.

"Sloane hates germs," says Asha.

"I know," says Lexi, and makes her mouth a tight line.

None of this makes sense. Asha understands that Sloane has had a crush on Connor for a long time and they're a couple now, and Lexi's lonely and wants to hang out with Joanna. But even so, why should Asha have to pay for Sloane's terrible judgment? It's so unfair.

"We can see each other another day," says Joanna.

But of course they can't. Winter break is starting this weekend, and Asha wanted to show her the drafting paper before that. And

Thursdays are their day. Because even after the break, Asha will still be busy on Mondays with tutoring and every other Wednesday with Dr. Wells and who knows what else, and the last thing Asha wants to do is explain her schedule to Joanna. But Thursdays work. Asha understands that Joanna loves sports, really she does, but there are other after-school sports on other days, like archery on Mondays and yoga on Wednesdays. Why can't Joanna do one of those?

"Or you could come to volleyball, too," says Joanna.

"I hate volleyball," says Asha. Well, it's true, she does. She's done a volleyball unit in gym for the last three years, and either it's completely boring because she's on the sidelines or it's completely miserable because she's on the court getting balls slammed at her. Even Sam understood that a sport where things come at you out of nowhere is just not fun. "It's such a stupid sport. My friend Sam hates it, too."

Joanna's eyes narrow. "Why do you call him that?"

"Call him what?"

"You always call Sam your friend. And he's not. He barely ever talks to you. He never sticks up for you with those girls. All he ever does is stand there or run away. Mostly just run away. But you always talk about him like he's so great. And he's not even nice."

The whole cafeteria dissolves away except for Joanna's

frowning face. It's not enough for her to ditch Asha; now she's trying to take Sam away, too. Why can't she understand that deep down Sam is still Asha's friend, even if he goes to Castleton and hangs out at Donnybrooke? They're just going through a rough patch. You can't know someone that well for that long and be their best friend—their *only* friend—and then just have the friendship disappear—*poof*—like it never happened. It can't work like that. It just can't.

Asha's chest hurts and the cafeteria noises sound distant, except for Lexi's swallowing, which is very, very loud. The air is getting thicker with each breath. Asha needs to leave. Now. She grabs her stuff and takes off at a run.

"I had a surprise for you," she says. But her words are lost to the din of seventh grade lunch.

The clouds hang low as Asha walks home. The sky is all wrong for mid-December. It's not quite fall and not quite winter. It's humid as summer, but there's supposed to be a cold front coming in. *The day doesn't fit anywhere*, Asha thinks, *just like me*.

She's mad at Joanna, but mostly she's mad at herself. She might have yelled in the cafeteria. She hates it when she does that. And she's not trying to be a bad friend. But Joanna knows that Thursday is the day that works for them, and she made plans anyway for all of the Thursdays for months from now.

Asha steps into her house and drops her backpack in her room. The drafting paper, untouched, is waiting on her desk. It's the last thing she wants to see right now. She needs something that will cheer her up, put her in the Christmas spirit.

And then it comes to her. Jolly. The giant old inflatable snowman they used to put up years ago. His white puffiness reminded Sam of astronaut suits. She runs into the basement, and sure enough, he's there in the holiday box, crumpled up along with some leftover tinsel and ornaments that didn't make the cut for the tree this year. She throws Jolly over her shoulder and goes back outside.

She plugs Jolly in and he inflates quickly. He's still as cheery as ever, with his charcoal mouth and carrot nose, but he's shorter than she remembered. She stands back-to-back with him, puts her hand to the top of her head, and measures straight. She turns back around. She's up to the brim of his hat. How is it that she's gotten so big and doesn't have a single friend?

Because, she thinks, maybe Joanna was right about Sam.

No sooner does she have that thought than Sam appears on the sidewalk before her. He's in his green polo, walking fast, head down. Asha is so surprised, she almost falls back into Jolly.

"Sam! What are you doing here?" she says once she regains her balance. But she already knows the answer. He's not here to put up holiday decorations, even if he used to love Jolly even more than she did. Still, Asha waits for him to talk or smile or even slow down.

Sam glances back over his shoulder, and Asha follows his gaze. Coming up the hill behind him are Prestyn and Tessa. Of course.

"I can't believe you think Prestyn the Intestine is nice," she says.

Sam still doesn't say anything.

"I stuck up for you today. At lunch, a girl was saying you're mean and I got mad at her for you. Because you're my friend." Asha is staring hard at him, but Sam won't look back.

Prestyn and Tessa have caught up to them now and are holding on to each other, giggling. "Awww, that's so sweet. 'You're my friend,'" says Prestyn, mimicking Asha's voice. "Can I be your friend, too, Asha?"

This is Sam's chance. To stay. To speak up. To prove Joanna wrong.

But he doesn't do any of those things. He runs away. Just like Joanna says he always does.

Sam

What Sam needs is another path to Prestyn's. One that doesn't take him by Asha's house. One that doesn't make him run into Jolly the Snowman by surprise and bring back all those memories that make his stomach feel weird. And definitely one that doesn't make Prestyn ask all these questions in her annoyed voice. If he could just teleport from the bus stop to Donnybrooke, everything would be so much easier. Instead he hasn't even put all his stuff away in the front closet and Prestyn is already after him.

"Did you tell Asha I wasn't nice? Why are you even over here if you think that? Do you and Asha still call me Prestyn the Intestine behind my back?"

"No," says Sam. "I don't even talk to her anymore."

Sam is glad that the bar stools in Donnybrooke let him spin away from Prestyn and Tessa. He expected this afternoon to be like last Thursday, when he and Prestyn made silly faces in the elevator mirrors and laughed and went up and down so many times he lost count, and it almost felt like they were friends. But now, from the moment he walked in, Prestyn seems to be mad at him even though he didn't call her any names at all.

Sam opens up Househaunt and pulls up his largest colonial, way larger than the one he actually lives in. It's time to build out that finished attic. The original plan was to have Asha do it for him, but the last thing he wants to do is ask her for help. So it's up to him. He scrolls through the room choices and picks the home office that's bound to have the best weapons. He could use more power. But as soon as he drops in the office, he realizes it's lit as if there's a skylight, but the outside of his house doesn't show any. And it's so big that it blocks off half the staircase. And it has no dormers and it should have two. Ugh. Those mistakes are sure to spawn hordes of At-ticks. And sure enough, within seconds, they start pouring out of the baseboards. Luckily Sam has matches.

He lights one, and a few At-ticks back off, but more emerge— and shoot!—they're carrying the At-tick Fana-tick on their shoulders. It's wearing a gold crown and holding a fat straw for slurping blood. Sam knows his mistakes were kind of big, but At-tick Fana-tick level? That doesn't seem fair. Of course, if Sam does manage to defeat it, he'll get three extra lives and a new wing on his house, and be in an elite class of monster-bug fighters. This could be his chance. He does have almost the entire box of matches.

"Are you bored?" asks Prestyn.

Sam lights four matches at once. The At-tick Fana-tick eases itself to the floor and starts lumbering toward him, two legs on the ground, six more reaching for him.

"I said, are you bored?"

Sam lights four more matches. He's never gone after the At-tick Fana-tick with this much firepower, and it's slowing down. Maybe that's all he needs to do. Keep lighting matches. Of course each one increases the risk of the whole house burning down, so he'll have to be careful.

"I'm talking to you." Prestyn swipes the phone right out of Sam's hands.

"Give it back!" yells Sam.

"Not until you answer me."

"Give it back!"

Prestyn glances at his phone. "Wait, is that thing . . . sucking all your blood . . . with a smoothie straw?"

Sam rushes to look over her shoulder. His avatar is turning white, and the At-tick Fana-tick is swelling right before his eyes. And now it's too late. He's dead. The game switches into aerial view as the Fana-tick takes him up to the roof and starts spinning him around. The Zombies on the ground wave their hands in the air, each hoping that it'll be the one to catch him and suck out his brain. As the At-tick Fana-tick releases him, it lets out a long, loud burp.

"Eeewww!" squeals Tessa.

Prestyn laughs and drops Sam's phone on the counter behind her.

"Why did you take my phone?" asks Sam. That wasn't right, even if the At-tick Fana-tick would have gotten him anyway.

"Why didn't you answer me when I asked if you were bored?"

"I wasn't bored. I was playing Househaunt."

Prestyn sighs, and Sam wonders why he always manages to say the wrong thing. "Not bored with your phone. Bored with us."

"I'm not bored with you," says Sam. He played on his phone the last time and Prestyn was fine with it.

"It's OK. It's not like we're doing anything. I'm bored, too. Aren't you bored, Tessa?"

"Uh . . . I think I'm fine, thanks."

"Aren't you always Little Miss Manners?" Prestyn laughs. "You can say you're bored. It's OK."

"I don't know. Maybe a little," says Tessa.

Prestyn nods. "We should play a game."

Sam *was* just playing a game. A pretty cool game, which he would show them if they asked, but they never do. They're not interested in Househaunt or any of the stuff he says about space or even the Medieval Life project that they all were supposed to do together. It's pretty annoying. But, Sam reminds himself, it's worth it, especially now. When Prestyn invites him over, kids leave him alone, he can pretend he's Castleton material, and he has a chance of making it to spring break. And his last time here, he and Prestyn even had fun.

"I have an idea!" says Prestyn. "Let's play hide-and-seek."

A chill cuts through the air. "No," says Sam.

Prestyn huffs. "Is this still about the elevator? Because I showed you, it's been fixed. Or do you want to take more kiddie rides?"

She and Tessa giggle. Sam feels his face flush. He thought Prestyn had fun on the elevator, too, making those goofy faces and pressing all the buttons. Why did she have to go tell Tessa about it?

"I'm kidding, I'm kidding," says Prestyn, putting her hands up like she's surrendering. Then she grabs Sam's arm. He jumps in shock as she pulls him off the bar stool. "Come on. It'll be fun," she says, marching him toward the elevator. Sam wonders if this is how it feels to be sucked into a black hole.

"I don't want—"

"I'll be It. Would that make you feel better?" Prestyn's fingers loosen on his arm.

"I can be It, too. I don't mind," says Tessa.

"No," says Prestyn. "I'll be It. It's only fair since I'm the one·

who wants to play. You guys can hide. Or not hide." She turns to Sam and smiles. "You can even just go back to your little bar stool and spin around if you'd like."

"No, I'll hide," says Sam. Now that it's a choice, he doesn't mind so much. Black hole averted. And they did take all those elevator rides. And it worked. And they had fun. More fun than he's had with any other Castleton kid. He doesn't want to be a bad sport, and he doesn't want to go back to how it is when Prestyn is mad at him. And he doesn't even have to hide if he changes his mind.

"Good," says Prestyn. They're in front of the elevator door now. As Tessa reaches for the button, Prestyn blocks her arm and smiles at Sam. "Why don't you give it a try?"

He presses the button and the machinery whirs. After a beat, the call light goes off and Prestyn opens the door. Sam takes a step forward.

"Wait!" says Prestyn. She shuts the door. "Press it again, Sam."

He does, and the button lights up again. They go through this routine two more times before Prestyn says to Sam, "See, it works just like last week. Happy now?"

"Yes," he says, following her onto the elevator. Prestyn is being really flexible and he appreciates it. Maybe today will be as fun as the last time.

When they reach the top, Prestyn says, "Ready or not," before she even steps off.

"You have to count," says Sam.

"Of course I will. Those are the rules."

As the elevator descends, Tessa starts to say something, but then she stops. She starts and stops again, and before Sam can ask her what's going on, the elevator comes to a halt on the second floor. Tessa scurries off with a quick look back. Sam is tempted to follow her. He's only been on that level that one time at Prestyn's party, and it probably has some great hiding places. But Mr. and Mrs. Donaldson's room is up there, and just the idea of it creeps him out. Even if they are never here.

Sam gets off on the first floor instead. The elevator lets out onto a hall with closed doors that he'd rather not open. The kitchen is on the other side of the wall—he could just go there and spin around on the bar stool, like Prestyn said. It is pretty relaxing doing that.

But he knows she wants to play. And there are so many parts of this house where Sam can go. He just has to find one where he'll be hidden and comfortable. He heads down the spiral staircase to the basement. He knows it well enough that he won't have to worry about walking in somewhere he shouldn't be.

He pauses at the bottom of the stairs by the side door. Outside's an option, too. He's never really been out there, and he'd like to check it out. Explore. Like Neil Armstrong on the moon. Even if he's always felt more like a Michael Collins. Stuck out in orbit.

He jiggles the door handle and steps outside. Just before the door shuts, he catches it with his foot. There's a small garden bed filled with smooth-edged stones, and he picks up a few. One of them is almost rectangular, like a miniature soap, and he makes a fist around it. Then he slips it in the door jamb. It fits like a missing puzzle piece. There, now he won't lock himself out. Prestyn and Tessa would laugh so hard at him if he did.

He runs around to the back of the house. There's a pool there, covered with a tarp for the season. Dead leaves are scattered on top. The wind picks up, cool and clean, and a few start to swirl like they're alive again. Zombie leaves, thinks Sam.

"Found you!" yells Prestyn from up high. She's on the roof deck, pointing down at him. Her voice is funny mixing with the wind.

Should he have done a better job hiding? That is part of the game. All the leaves around him are doing the zombie dance now.

"You didn't hide," says Prestyn. "You're bored, aren't you?"

"No," says Sam. He wishes she'd quit saying that. He hasn't been bored since getting off the bus this afternoon. Not that he'd care if he was. "I just wanted to be outside."

"Really?" says Prestyn. "In this weather?"

"Yes," says Sam. "I wanted—"

"Doesn't matter," says Prestyn. "Because you're It!"

Donnybrooke

Eyeing the Storm

The elevator stops at the roof deck. The noise of the jabbering trees fills the space. Prestyn raises her voice over them. "Remember, count all the way to forty, no matter what. We'll know if you cheated."

The boy steps off slowly. Tessa's eyes are strangely shiny, and she starts coughing loudly. It's an unsettling sound.

"See you . . . when we see you," says Prestyn.

The door shuts.

The boy counts.

It wouldn't hurt him to go a bit faster. This game is tricky enough in fair weather, and this weather isn't fair. The wind is strengthening; the sky is menacing. The sluggish clouds that sit over Donnybrooke fall off into a sharp darkness to the west. It's the kind of sky that means business, bringing storms

and cold and rousing the trees. And indeed, now they're up and at it. This is how it is with the trees. They're either all silent and still, or they're blowing as one. For not the first time, Donnybrooke wonders: What would it be like to have so many others in sync with you? You might never know how loneliness feels.

The trees are gossiping about Donnybrooke now. Why? They have everything: they grow and change with the seasons; they always have companions. They could spare a little compassion for the mansion. It's not Donnybrooke's fault it was built the way it was, any more than it's Donnybrooke's fault that the boy is on its roof deck right now. Yet the trees are shaking with blame. Don't they realize Donnybrooke only has the power it's given?

Oh!

No!

But why, Prestyn? Why?

The trees begin to hiss as the hard blue sky advances. It's as if they know what's just happened inside the utility room, too, and they're ready to punish Donnybrooke for it. In less than a minute, they've launched an all-out assault. They spit cold and leaves in all directions, clogging the gutters and drains. The boy covers his face with his arms and runs to the elevator vestibule, yelling, "Forty! Forty!"

He presses the button once. It stays dark. He presses it again. Nothing. He is quiet, and for a moment the trees are, too, but Donnybrooke isn't fooled. The silence is heavy with rage, and the rage is aimed right at Donnybrooke. But Donnybrooke would give anything to be able to protect the boy the way any other home in Coreville could. Anything. But its energy is drained. Prestyn has made sure of that.

The boy shivers. Then his finger is out, jabjabjabjab, right on the button as fast as he can. So hard it could jam. It doesn't, though.

He lets out a bark of rage. The trees join in. He kicks the elevator doors hard.

Donnybrooke can't even be mad at him for that.

A window opens. Does he hear the crack? Or the voices?

"Seriously, Pressie, this is the stinkiest polish ever!"

"You're the one who wanted a mani."

He runs to the east side railing and holds on tight. It's the closest he's ever been to the edge. "Let me down!" he yells. "I have to go home! And it's cold out here."

"Try zipping up your jacket!" yells Prestyn. "Oh, wait, you left it inside."

She shuts the window before she stops laughing.

"Help!" he yells. "I need help!"

Why would they do that, Prestyn and her friend? This isn't

the time. The boy is telling the truth like he always does. It's getting colder by the minute, and the trees are in a dangerous mood. They're liable to hurl whatever they can: twigs, branches, even themselves. And the wind is a force of fury, tearing at every crack and flaw in the deck itself. Donnybrooke just wants to ferry the boy down and be done with this whole day. But it can't. The girls have seen to that. They've made it worse than useless.

They've made it their weapon.

How could the girls do this? Have they forgotten that Donnybrooke is first and foremost a house? What's the point of all the columns, spare rooms, and turrets—of being a so-called "mansion"—if Donnybrooke can't even shelter the people inside it? That's the most basic function of a home. The most important. And now Donnybrooke is literally powerless to keep the boy safe.

The trees are up in arms, roaring about the injustice of it all. They're so busy with their righteous indignation, they've forgotten about the actual boy who is huddled on the splintering roof deck, freezing. To the west, the slate sky continues its advance. The darkness is only broken by a flash of lightning.

The boy needs to get down. Nature is not on his side.

Sam

Sam hates heights. They make his legs shake and his stomach wobble and his head spin. But now, even more than heights, Sam hates the wind. It's like an icy Witch-One slashing at his face and arms. How is it possible he came up here in short sleeves?

He jogs in place and tries to rub away his goose bumps. He doesn't let himself look down. He can picture his phone on the mottled marble counter where Prestyn dropped it. He clenches his teeth together. He's not going to cry this time. He's not.

He jogs faster. He can survive this at least for another minute or two. He tries to think about spring break. How warm it will be at the Kennedy Space Center. Even if it is windy.

But it's hard to imagine Florida. He isn't even sure how he's going to get off this roof. Why is Prestyn acting like this is a big joke? Doesn't she get how scary it is up here? How much trouble he'll be in if he doesn't get home on time? His mom will call the school and find out he's not at soccer—*never* was at soccer—and she'll realize all the stuff about him being Castleton material was one big lie. That he never deserved the soccer cupcakes or a Space Center trip. That she was proud of him for nothing.

"Help!" he yells. "You have to help, Prestyn!" It's hard to think of anything else to say.

The only response is a flash in the sky. Sam freezes. He waits. He really thinks he saw a flash, though. Maybe he blinked funny. God, he hopes that's it, and not a storm coming in. Thunder would be even worse than the wind. And lightning worse than thunder, even if they technically are the same thing.

"Prestyn?" he says. It's hardly a whisper. Why would it be more? She's not coming anyway. She put him here in the first place. She's leaving him on purpose. Every time she's "saved" him, he's only needed saving because he trusted her enough to do what she said. And even then she's taken her time.

He can't wait for her to save him now.

He races to the other side of the roof. The deck feels shaky under his feet. He doesn't want to look up or down. The truth is, he doesn't need to. He knows what's there, over the fence, past the trees. Asha's house.

For just a moment, the air hushes.

And Sam screams again for the one person he trusts to save him after all.

"Asha! Asha! Asha!"

Asha

Poor Jolly wasn't made for this. Even with his electric motor, the wind is battering him this way and that. Asha can relate. That's how she's felt all afternoon.

As soon as Sam and Prestyn left, she texted Rohan about what happened, but even that didn't help. He replied right away, but with another one of his cryptic answers. She could practically see him stroking his scruffy beard.

Are you mad that you were nice to him?

Because you're not nice to him because of who he is.

You're nice to him because of who you are.

That's who you want to be.

Even if he didn't use his fancy words, he still didn't give her any real advice. He didn't tell her how to make Sam be her friend again, or how to show him how awful Prestyn is, or how to make up with Joanna. Rohan gave her a complete nonanswer, which is even worse than a bad answer because those at least cheer her up for a while before she realizes they're wrong. Instead she's been puzzling over his nonanswer texts for close to an hour, but they still don't make sense. She's not at all sure she wants to be who she is. What has it gotten her? She'd much rather be lucky like Prestyn.

The wind kicks up higher. It's louder than Jolly's weak motor and attacks everything in its path: the humidity, Jolly, even Asha herself. She covers her face with her arms as a swell of leaves come at her like a mass of cicadas. It's time to go inside. Between the wind and the dark sky, it could start pouring any minute. There's nothing like a storm to make her love the shelter of her own home.

She darts to the outdoor socket. With a quick pull of the plug, Jolly deflates, and she rushes to get him before the wind does. But strangely, it dies down, too.

In the quiet, she hears the yelling. Sam. Straight from the top of Donnybrooke.

"Asha!"

He's scared. And he's calling for her.

But he's not her friend. Not anymore. The worst thing about what Joanna said was that it was true. Rohan thinks so, too. If there's anything she got from his texts, it's that.

Sam calls again. *"Ashaaaaa! Ashaaaaa!"*

Asha looks to Donnybrooke, the turret tops and the weather vane hard and pointed in the advancing dark.

"Help!"

The winds start up again, drowning out anything else Sam might be saying. A gust tugs at Jolly, and Asha has to hug him hard to keep him from flying away. She yanks opens the storm door and drops Jolly between it and the real door. The snowman, at least, is safe.

But Sam isn't.

Asha runs. She knows she shouldn't. She promised her mom and dad. But the wind is screeching like there's worse to come, and Sam sounds like an animal that's been orphaned. Asha can help him. She just needs to be fast. Maybe what Rohan was saying isn't that stupid. Because right now Asha doesn't care if they'll ever make up or if Sam should have been a better friend or if he'd do the same for her. This isn't about who Sam is. It's about who Asha is.

The gates of Donnybrooke are locked. Asha doesn't bother shaking them. Instead she drops down onto her stomach and turns her head for a freestyle breath. Her head's in, then her shoulder, then her—oh, no!—her middle is stuck! She wriggles and writhes. She can't let herself think about what would happen if she were found like that. She absolutely can't. She sucks in her stomach hard and yanks at her jacket. She might have heard a rip. But it's OK because she's in!

Oh, no. She's in. She'd better be fast. Her hair whips across her face as she runs up the driveway. The windows in the front of the house are dark, like the many eyes of a sleeping spider. Asha doesn't want to be there when they wake up. She slips under the eaves and creeps with her back against the wall. It's rougher than it looks, and once or twice the fabric of her jacket catches, as if Donnybrooke wants to hold her back. She hopes the wind is drowning out whatever noise her feet might make.

Heart in throat, she steps out from under the eaves. "Sam!"

She waits. And waits. Maybe he couldn't hear her.

"Sam!" she says, louder this time. She claps her hand to her mouth and ducks back under the eaves.

"Asha? You're here?"

"You were yelling again."

"I'm cold. She always makes me so cold."

His voice and his words make everything about this awful moment even worse, and Asha has to laugh to let some of the stress of it out. She inhales sharply.

"You have to get down."

"I know. But I can't."

Asha forces herself to breathe again. The wind is stinging her face. "Take the elevator down."

"I can't."

"You can."

"It doesn't work."

"How did you get up there?"

"It only works when they take me up."

That makes no sense. An elevator can't just work in one direction. Unless . . . unless . . . Prestyn is turning it off on purpose. Maybe that's her secret. It's much easier to be lucky when you're the one in control.

Asha leans against the wall of the house, away from the sharp bits of blowing leaf and debris. This isn't a problem she can solve for him. She reaches for her phone to call her mom. But it isn't there. She must have left it at home. After all, she hadn't planned to come.

"I'm going home. I'm going to call your mom," says Asha.

"No! She thinks I'm at soccer."

"She still thinks that?"

"Yes. If she finds out I'm here, I'll be in so much trouble."

"You're already in trouble."

"Don't, Asha. Please. She can't know. And I can't wait that long."

The sky flashes, as if to agree.

"I've got to go," says Asha. She's beginning to sweat underneath her jacket, cold and hot at the same time. Why is she under the eaves when she wants more than anything to be under the plush fleece blankets on her bed?

"Asha, wait! Do you know how to turn the elevator back on?"

Of course she knows how. Like that's a question.

"I left the side door unlocked. It'll only take a second."

She can't. Why would he ask her to do that?

"Prestyn's mom—" says Asha.

"She's not here. She's never here when I'm over. Please." Sam's voice shakes at the end. He might be crying. "Asha?" pleads Sam.

Could she do it? It's scary, but maybe not impossible. She's worked on facing fears for long enough that she knows there's no special trick to doing it other than doing it. But doing it is not easy.

Lightning splits the sky. She barely counts out two seconds before the thunder claps. Why does Sam have to be up by the weather vane—practically a lightning rod—right now? Asha bolts to the side door and presses her body against it. It gives like a soft spot on fruit.

Inside, the spiral staircase is almost dark. A light's burned out since she was last here, and her shadow is long across the wall. She can hear her own breathing, too loud in her ears, and then two voices from almost directly above her.

"Can we turn the elevator on already? Your house has too many stairs."

"It's good exercise. You can work off all the guac you ate."

Asha darts into the basement hallway, past a bathroom that oozes that lemon-lily smell, and into the utility room. She closes the door just before she hears footsteps approaching.

"What was that?"

Asha holds her breath and keeps her muscles so still they almost shake.

"What?"

"I think I might have heard him."

Prestyn laughs the same mean laugh she did at her party. It still makes Asha flinch. "Uh, I think he's a bit higher up than the basement."

"Maybe we shouldn't leave him out there."

"Maybe he shouldn't have called me Prestyn the Intestine." She laughs again.

"Pressie . . . that was a really long time ago. And I think we should let him down now. It's starting to storm."

"You're such a sap sometimes. He's fine."

Asha bites her lip and breathes. Sam is totally not fine, and Prestyn doesn't even care.

It's up to Asha.

Her eyes have adjusted enough to the darkness of the utility room to make out the sharp shapes of the fuse boxes. Asha creeps toward them on tiptoe, careful not to bump anything. From outside comes a long, low rumble, like distant thunder. Asha squints to find the latch.

"Oh, no! It's my mom," says Prestyn.

Asha freezes. The air around her and the blood inside her seem to as well. Her mind slowly processes her mistake. Garage door, not thunder. She should have known the difference.

"Hello?" Mrs. Donaldson's voice echoes in the basement hall. It's scratchy and hard and makes Asha want to stress-laugh, even though she's trying her best to stay hidden.

"Hi, Mom!" says Prestyn loudly.

"Why are you down here?"

Prestyn and Tessa start blabbering so fast it makes Asha's head spin, but she's still too scared to move. The scent of bleach and lemon-lily soap fills the utility room, stinging Asha's eyes and nose. She allows herself two blinks and one breath. Her flexed fingers begin to shake.

Thunder booms, definitely thunder this time. It's so loud that Asha thinks the lightning couldn't have been even a second before. Then a *rat-a-tat* of sticks and such hitting the house, and maybe Sam, too. She can't keep waiting. She pops the latch to the fuse box door. She can't read the ribbon labels in the darkness, but she brushes each one with her fingertips and counts.

She can picture the faded writing: *elevator*. Just one more over.

The utility room door swings open. Asha pulls back her hand like it's been burned.

"You!" screams Mrs. Donaldson as she switches on the light. Prestyn and Tessa run in behind her. All six of their horrified eyes drill into her. Asha clamps both of her hands over her face. She forces herself to breathe, in-out, in-out.

"Is this some attention-seeking trick, Prestyn?"

"No! I—I didn't even know she was here."

Mrs. Donaldson steps toward Asha and hisses, "I warned you. I warned you and your mother what would happen if you trespassed again. That's against the law."

Everything inside Asha is quaking and maybe outside her, too. Everything except for Mrs. Donaldson, who is carefully dialing on a candy-pink cell phone.

"What are you doing, Mom?"

"I'm calling the police. There's an intruder in my home."

At these words, any strength Asha had leaves her. She drops to the floor and curls into the smallest ball her body will make and breathes in the sweat and bleach and soap and the black coffee and whatever else Mrs. Donaldson drank this afternoon. Asha is trying to force back all the things she knows: that she is alone in this, that the storm is upon them, that Sam is stuck, that Prestyn put him there, that Asha not only can't help him but is about to be in more trouble than she ever has been in her whole life, and when that happens, everyone she loves, everyone who told her not to even think about Donnybrooke, is going to look at her just like Mrs. Donaldson does. She's trembling like a Househaunt house, overrun with monsters, past the point of saving, and she finally understands what it means to be condemned.

Donnybrooke

in Distress

This is all too much, too much for a house like Donny- brooke. It cannot help the boy. It cannot help itself. It's being battered and bruised. The trees are hurling sticks and branches in all directions. They've whipped themselves up into such a frenzy, they don't even realize they're hurting themselves as much as Donnybrooke. Meanwhile, sirens wail in the distance and lightning cracks and circles ever closer to the weather vane.

And yet the sounds inside are far worse. Mrs. Donaldson's relentless pacing. Asha's irregular hiccups. Prestyn's uneven gasps. She gets the words out as she can.

"Call them back, Mom! You have to. They can't come. They can't. They can't." Prestyn is shaking almost as much as the girl. That poor, poor girl.

"You're defending her?"

"No, I just . . . I just . . ." Prestyn's eyes are on the ceiling. Her mother has no idea about the boy, but Prestyn hasn't forgotten. Right now, he's crouching against the elevator vestibule, but it's simply not sized for shelter. Nowhere on the roof deck is, as Prestyn knows all too well. She drops her gaze to Asha.

"Why can't we just leave her alone?"

Yes. That's the question, the one Donnybrooke has had since the very beginning.

But Mrs. Donaldson narrows her eyes. "Leave *her* alone. She's the one who doesn't leave *us* alone. Walking by our house and staring at it. Ruining my party. Ruining your party. Lest you forget, Prestyn, this girl is the reason you cut off all your gorgeous, gorgeous hair."

"No, Mom, she's not. That's just what you wanted to hear. But no one made me. I did it myself." Prestyn is shaking her head, and her face is wet with tears. Her mother either doesn't notice or doesn't care. "But the police can't come now. They can't."

"Don't you remember what her mother did to me at our very first party here?"

"I was in the playroom. I only know because you won't stop talking about it."

"And look at her now. She's laughing at us still. She thinks this is funny."

"I don't think she does," says Tessa.

Mrs. Donaldson whips around as if she hadn't been aware of Tessa's presence. "And I don't think I asked you."

The doorbell rings. Finally something in Donnybrooke's circuitry is working as it should. Mrs. Donaldson takes Prestyn by the arm and marches her upstairs.

Tessa walks over to the circuit board and grabs a handful of labels. She reads them, one by one. Outside, the lightning and the wind continue to rage. Tessa takes another handful of labels and squints. There isn't time for this.

The loudest boom yet shakes them all.

"Help," Tessa whimpers.

Asha uncurls and rises. Donnybrooke knows she must be hurting inside as much as it is outside, but even so, she flips the switch with the sureness she's always had with her favorite home.

Asha

Any relief Asha feels vanishes as soon as Mrs. Donaldson enters the utility room with the police officer. He starts talking to Asha, but it's impossible to focus on what he's saying with Mrs. Donaldson baring her too-white teeth and all the smells and knowing what's about to happen.

The officer steps toward Asha, and Asha steps back, bumping the fuse box.

"Excuse me, miss. Could you please explain what you're doing here?"

No, she can't, not with Sam still up on the roof, and Mrs. Donaldson hovering over her. Asha covers her face with her hands and peeks through the cracks between her fingers.

"She's trespassing, obviously," says Mrs. Donaldson.

"No, she's not," says Tessa. "We invited her. She's our friend."

Asha opens her fingers a little wider and stares at Tessa. It's such a strange thing for her to say. Tessa is Prestyn's friend, not Asha's. Asha doesn't have any friends anymore. But why would Tessa lie? Is she trying to help Asha somehow? It's impossible to figure out for sure because Mrs. Donaldson and Prestyn and Tessa have all started yelling at one another.

"Please!" says the officer. "I'd like to hear directly from the girl about why she's here."

Tessa starts nodding at Asha, her eyes large like she's trying not to blink, and she's biting the inside of her cheeks so hard she's making a fish face. Beside her, Prestyn is shaking her head no, but Tessa keeps nodding anyway. She's on Asha's side.

Asha slows her breathing. "Sam. I came for Sam."

"Sam? Sam? She's making things up! There's no Sam—" starts Mrs. Donaldson.

"Please," says the officer.

"Sam's on the roof. He's stuck."

"Is Sam a pet?" asks the officer.

"No," says a hoarse voice from the elevator that makes Asha dizzy with relief. "It's me."

But before the officer can ask another question, before Mrs. Donaldson can shriek in shock, before Prestyn can let out a sob, a crash shakes the walls so hard that Asha thinks this really might be the end, if not of her, then of Donnybrooke.

Donnybrooke

Missing Something

Oh, Donnybrooke is still standing. It is. It is. But . . .

The *weather vane*. Its weather vane broke last night.

To be sure, it's not like the walls crumbled or the roof caved in. Its deck, though damaged, didn't collapse. But the weather vane. It was supposed to be the one part of Donnybrooke that was truly invincible: a steel eagle ready to strike. It never occurred to Donnybrooke that some well-timed electricity along with wind and wood could defeat it. It never knew that the softest elements can hold the most strength.

What more is there to say? Donnybrooke believed the stories the Donaldsons told. That what mattered most was impressing others. Show over shelter. Size equals strength. That the wealth of their home could protect them from hurt.

That it was even possible to be better than everyone else. Life seemed so much clearer if those things were true.

The school called first thing this morning. Apparently the boy's family told them about all of the ugliness of last night, and there was a question about whether Prestyn should return. But Mr. Donaldson got on his phone with his lawyer, a lady with a fast mouth and strong lungs. She came over lickety-split, attempted to chat with Prestyn (who, granted, wasn't in much of a mood to talk), and then called the school right back, throwing around phrases like *lack of jurisdiction*, *prior notice*, and *site of the last five fundraising campaign kickoffs*. As far as Donnybrooke can tell, none of those things have anything to do with leaving a boy out in a storm on purpose. But they worked. By lunch, Prestyn had resumed her studies at Castleton.

And after she was squared away, the next thing on the Donaldsons' list was Donnybrooke. Not the roof deck cracks or stairs—they may never get to those—just the broken weather vane. And so, within the hour, the most visible piece of Donnybrooke will be removed. It's telling itself this is all for the best, this speedy "repair."

It's just . . . it's just that Donnybrooke has never been a house without it. Logically, yes, Donnybrooke knows the weather vane was simply decorative, and not actually a symbol of everything it stood for. But deep down, that eagle dominating the skyline felt like the essence of what made Donnybrooke unique . . . what made it notable . . . what made it envied.

It's true, even the trees knew it: Donnybrooke wanted to inspire envy.

It seemed like the closest it could get to love.

Sam

Last night at Donnybrooke, everyone had a question for Sam.

Mrs. Donaldson: "What on earth are you doing here?"

The police officer: "How long were you stuck up there?"

Asha and, weirdly, Tessa: "Are you OK?"

Sam's answer was the same for all of them: "I don't know."

Sam's mom had the most questions, though she didn't even try to ask them until he was at home in his room.

"How come—?"

"How long—?"

"Why didn't—?"

Then, finally, a statement: "I thought you were at soccer."

For once in this terrifying, tumultuous evening, Sam had complete clarity. "No. I never was at soccer. I hate it. I've always hated it." Then he marched to his closet and popped open the planetarium umbrella.

As he sat underneath its stars, he heard his mother gulp hard. "But I always thought . . . I mean, I never thought . . . Oh, Sammy . . . I'm sorry."

Sam wakes up this morning with some of last night's cold still lingering in his bones and a soreness that's settled in his ears. He checks his clock. School has already started. For a second, he thinks that maybe it's already the weekend. But no, it's Friday. There's still one day left before winter break. He imagines being at Castleton, and everyone laughing at him for being dumb enough to get stuck on the roof deck. Sure, Prestyn and Tessa weren't laughing when they saw him last night, but who knows what they'd do today? They always do whatever they feel like. Sam shuts his eyes. He can't go back to school today.

When he finally gets out of bed, both his mom and dad are downstairs, and it turns out he does have to go to school, just not until after dismissal. They have a meeting with Dr. Deutsch.

"She sounds like she wants to help," says his mom.

"No way," mutters Sam.

"Yeah, I'm not sure about that. But you might as well relax in the meantime," says his dad.

Sam tries to take that advice. But even though he plays

Househaunt and watches old *Cosmos* reruns, he can't help but think about last night and Prestyn and Tessa and how all of it comes back to Castleton. By the time three o'clock rolls around, he'd give anything not to go.

"C'mon, Sammy, it'll be OK," says his mom.

Sam is sure now that she doesn't know what she's talking about. If he had more energy, he might actually tell her that.

They arrive at Castleton just after the dismissal bell. Sam stares at the ground and tries to hide behind his dad as they walk in, but no one seems to notice he's there. For once, being ignored is a relief. As they pass the eighth grade honor guards, Sam's dad glances at the school flags and mutters, "Snakes? How appropriate!" loud enough that one of the honor guards starts giggling so hard that she lets the flag touch the ground and then has to kiss it. Even though Sam does not want to be here, he does smile at that.

Dr. Deutsch is already waiting for them when they get to her office. Her glasses, as usual, are perched on her head. They have an iridescent coating on them that makes them look like soap bubbles just before they burst. Sam focuses on them as he sits wedged between his parents.

"Before we get started in earnest, I just have a few factual questions for Sam," says Dr. Deutsch. She leans toward him and props her glasses on her nose. "Did any incidents with Prestyn Donaldson occur on school property? Did you complain, orally or in writing, to any Castleton teachers or administrators? Were you ever assigned to work with her despite requesting not to?"

Sam keeps shaking his head. He doesn't understand these questions. He thinks he knows what they mean, but he definitely doesn't know what they have to do with his experience at Castleton. Which is something he has a lot of questions about. Like, *What about all the kids who acted like I was invisible? What about all the teachers who did nothing about that? What about Alec and his crowd and all of their "Miracle Boy" stupidity? What about you, Dr. Deutsch, for starting it all?* All of that seems way more relevant.

Sam's dad apparently agrees because he says in that forced-calm voice he saves for his work calls, "Is this truly about trying to figure out how to move forward? Or is it about how to limit your liability? Because it sure sounds like the latter."

Dr. Deutsch clears her throat. It's a fake sound, like her throat isn't really itchy. "Very well then, let's talk about what's next. I have to say, this is a tough situation. You've alleged some pretty bad behavior by one of Sam's fellow students, and as a school, we have to think about the big picture. Whether it makes sense for these children to continue to be educated together."

Sam's mother gives his hand a quick squeeze. Her palm is

sweaty. Sam really hopes Dr. Deutsch speeds up so they can go soon. But if anything, her voice gets slower and syrupier.

"The biggest question, of course, is what's best for Sam."

"Of course," says his mom, giving Sam another squeeze. He pulls his hand away and sits on it.

"And as we discussed last year, he's a bright boy. But he's not a typical candidate for admission here. Maybe that's something we should have looked at more closely."

"Excuse me? Could you please clarify?" says his dad, still using his work-call voice.

Sam sinks in his chair, wishing it were a portal to another galaxy. Why does his dad need clarification? Dr. Deutsch is saying something is wrong with him. Even his mom knows that. She's shifting so much in her seat that it's making Sam's wobble.

"I believe we discussed that even though Sam has a number of strengths, his profile is unlike that of the other students here, and that could be causing certain difficulties."

Sam's mom turns pale. When she speaks, her voice is shaking. "Tell me you are not saying what I think you're saying."

Sam's dad reaches over and touches her arm. "Again, just to clarify, are you referring to the fact that he's on the autism spectrum?" he says. Sam's chest tightens, and next to him, his mom goes still. His parents never say those words out loud if they can help it.

"Well, yes, I suppose I am."

"Because, as I'm sure you're aware, Castleton Academy is covered by the Americans with Disabilities Act, so that's illegal," says his dad.

"Which means Sam isn't the one with a problem here. You are," says Sam's mom in her *I'm not yelling* voice, which Sam would argue actually is a yell. All the anger Sam imagined she'd have about soccer appears to be laser-focused on Dr. Deutsch.

Dr. Deutsch's mouth drops open. She's speechless. It's almost worth returning to Castleton just to see that.

"Now that's not . . . I didn't . . . I think you misunderstood me . . . I . . . I believed Sam could be our miracle boy as much as anyone."

Miracle Boy.

The words cut straight to Sam's gut. He never wanted to be a miracle boy. He just wanted to learn some cool stuff, meet some fun kids, and visit the planetarium. But he never had the chance.

"You messed everything up!" says Sam.

Dr. Deutsch peers at him, her eyes as cold as last night's wind. "Now I'll have to ask you to use a calm voice. And to be clear, I've only tried to help you."

"Help me? With all that 'Miracle Boy' garbage?"

"Now, Sam. I called you a Castleton Star. It's not fair to blame me if things haven't worked out. All sorts of kids aren't Castleton material. There's no shame in that."

"How dare you? Sam is smart and he's curious and—" As his mom launches into a list of all the things she thinks he is, Sam thinks about the thing he definitely isn't.

"—determined and inquisitive and—"

"I'm not—" interrupts Sam.

"You are every one of those things and more," snaps his mom.

"I'm not Castleton material. All the kids here act like being mean to each other and ignoring other kids is more fun than playing games or talking about space or houses or whatever. Why would I want to be like that?"

None of the grown-ups respond. His mom trembles a bit, like she's trying not to cry or, possibly, strangle Dr. Deutsch. His dad swallows loudly, like he's forcing down his words. Dr. Deutsch fake-clears her throat over and over, but even she doesn't say anything.

"Can we go now?" says Sam. "I hate this place."

Sam leads the way out of Dr. Deutsch's office, past the flagpole, and to the parking lot. He remembers the burst of happiness when he learned he'd been accepted to Castleton. He felt like he'd finally done something right, something that mattered. He takes a long look at the planetarium dome and tries to think of one good day he had here. He can't. He's not sure what leaving will mean for his future, but he knows what it means for now. He doesn't need anyone else to tell him he's made the right choice.

His mom catches up to him as they reach the car. "Sam, I'm so sorry. About Castleton. About talking to that reporter. About not noticing what you were going through. I've been worrying about all the wrong things."

"You know how you said my issues were a part of me but they almost didn't matter? But shouldn't all of me matter?" asks Sam.

His parents nod, slow at first, but then faster.

"Yup," his dad says.

Asha

Asha is glad for the winter break. She needs the time and space to recover. Mostly she does that by hanging out with Rohan. They watch movies and play Househaunt, and he teaches her some coding he's learned in college. When her cousins come to visit, they mull apple cider and bake Christmas cookies, and the whole family takes long winter walks all over the neighborhood. Anywhere they go, they can see Donnybrooke.

But it's different now. The weather vane is gone, of course, so there's no eagle lording over them or the rest of Coreville. Asha wonders about the fish, though. It'll be in a landfill somewhere with those talons just an inch from grabbing it. And it'll take a long, long time—maybe millennia—to decompose.

"I still feel bad for the Donnybrooke fish," she tells her mom, who's fallen in step next to her.

"I think I feel bad for that whole place," says her mom.

They talk about Donnybrooke now, what happened the first time there and all the times since. Asha finally believes her mom that she didn't do anything wrong either, that time when she was little—after all, Sam didn't do anything wrong, and look what happened to him. People have all sorts of reasons for doing things, and usually it's more about them than you. At least that's what Asha's mom said. That and, "I shouldn't have asked you not to think or care about Donnybrooke. What you think and feel makes you you." Asha can admit to loving Donnybrooke as much as she wants now.

The only thing is, she doesn't anymore. Even as she looks up at it, she doesn't dream of waking up under a turreted ceiling or sliding down a spiral banister. She doesn't imagine how lucky she would feel to host a party there or come home every day through those enormous gates. Because there's nothing lucky about being the kind of person who makes Sam scream and Asha shake with fear, and there's nothing lucky about a house where that happens.

Fat snowflakes start to fall, and Asha can't help but think of the cherry blossom petals that swirled around her in Sam's tree. Everything seemed to change in that moment, and now everything has changed again. She wanted so much to stay his friend. And every day since she saved him, she's been less and less sure she ever wants to see him again. She picks up her pace until she's beside Rohan leading the way up Maplevale Lane.

"Can I ask you a question?"

"If I can ask you one. But you go first," he says.

"I'm so mad at Sam. I didn't even know I could be this mad at him. And I feel bad about it. Like I shouldn't be."

"That's your question?"

She nods, and some of the melted snow from her hair drips down her scalp.

Rohan folds his arms across his chest. "The only way not to be mad at him is to be mad at him for as long as you need to be."

"Uggghhh." Asha wishes there were enough snow to chuck a snowball at her brother.

"What?"

"Just give me a normal answer."

"He put you in a really bad position and wasn't a good friend for months, and that's way worse than doing volleyball on Thursdays. Is that a normal answer?"

"Yeah, thanks," says Asha. "That's what I'm thinking, too."

"Now it's my turn." He looks over his shoulder as if to make sure no one else can hear him. Then he says in a low voice, "Do you still think this beard makes me look silly, and not any older?"

"That's what I think, but it's your face."

"The problem is I've spent nine months trying to convince

myself you're wrong, and I haven't been able to. So, I have another question for you. Will you laugh at me if I shave it off?"

Asha giggles. "No! We can bake something to celebrate."

"Then preheat the oven because it's time for me to shave."

They high-five by the front door. Then Asha turns the key, and they walk into the warmth of their house together.

Winter break ends much too soon. Asha could spend forever sleeping in, eating cookies for breakfast, and never setting foot in the Sullivan Middle School cafeteria. But before she knows it, it's noon on January 2, and she's forcing herself to walk to lunch. As she stalls by the cafeteria doors, Joanna comes up beside her.

"Hi, Asha," she says.

"Hi!" Asha takes a deep breath, but her mind is racing. Before she can lose her nerve, she says, "I'm sorry about yelling at you. You were right about Sam, and it's totally fine if you like volleyball. Do you like volleyball?"

Joanna nods eagerly.

"A lot?"

Joanna nods again.

"Well, if you're not mad at me, maybe you can come over another time, like on the weekend or something. I still have your surprise."

"You do? I can't wait!" says Joanna. Then she raises her eyebrows and points to their table. "Speaking of surprises . . ."

Sloane is sitting next to Lexi like she never left. Connor is nowhere in sight.

"Why aren't you with Connor?" asks Asha as she puts down her lunch box. "I thought you liked him."

"It's complicated." Sloane sighs dramatically. "We got together over break a few times and I just . . . I don't know . . ." She primly puts her napkin on her lap. "I guess I realized you all have much better table manners."

You didn't need to go out with Connor to figure that out, thinks Asha. But she says, "It's OK. Everyone makes mistakes."

Donnybrooke

Waiting for the Thaw

It's the dead of winter outside and in. Donnybrooke keeps waiting for a sign of a thaw, a hint that its family will soften and be the way they should have been all along. But when Mrs. Donaldson returns from grocery shopping, slams the bag on the kitchen counter, and storms upstairs, it's clear the freeze isn't relenting today.

Mrs. Donaldson enters Prestyn's room without knocking. "I ran into Addison's mother at Coreville Farmcart this afternoon. She was very smug. Do you know what she said about you?"

Prestyn turns over so her back is facing her mother. "I don't care." Her voice shakes unconvincingly.

Mrs. Donaldson lets out a harsh laugh. "Well, maybe if you cared a little more, you wouldn't have gotten yourself in this

mess. Really, after everything I've done to make you happy. And all you can do is lie there."

Instead of fighting back, Prestyn goes stiff like the icicles on the eaves, not moving until a tear rolls down her cheek. Then she lifts a throw pillow—one of the white satin ones—and presses her face to it.

Mrs. Donaldson says, "Oh, stop being so dramatic. You'll stain the pillow."

It's true that Prestyn's behavior was deeply disappointing, and the subsequent gossip is, of course, quite embarrassing. But now, as Prestyn trembles in her bed, Donnybrooke can't help but wonder if it loves her more than her own mother.

An hour later, when Mr. Donaldson returns home, Mrs. Donaldson's mood has not improved. She frowns at him, and his face hardens. Donnybrooke braces for them to start arguing about one of their usual topics: the money they spend (or don't), how much they see family (or not), how much he's home (or not). And lately what to do about Prestyn. But today Mrs. Donaldson has a different target: DONNYBROOKE!

"It's a lot of house for just the three of us," she says.

"The maintenance is a real pain," she says.

"It's starting to feel dated," she says.

Dated? Dated! Could she be more insulting? But then she

says, "The layout never really worked, you know."

Never? Never! Donnybrooke was her dream house! She picked the layout. She suggested the modifications. There are blueprints rolled up in the attic with notes in her handwriting. She created Donnybrooke. And now she is forsaking Donnybrooke when all it ever did was be what she wanted it to be.

Mr. Donaldson says nothing to defend it. He retreats to his office turret and studies the pictures of his glory days at the Stonebury School. Does he even notice that he's in a room built just for him?

Donnybrooke is still smarting when Mr. Donaldson knocks on Prestyn's door after dinner with a brochure in his hand. She is on her phone, scrolling absently. When he enters, she perches on the edge of her bed. He pauses for a moment before putting the brochure down and sitting next to her. It's strange to see the two of them together like this. Usually they each keep to their own turret.

Prestyn breaks the silence. "What do you want?"

"Can't I just want to catch up with my kid?" He plasters a goofy grin on his face and pats her back awkwardly.

"You haven't tried to have a real conversation with me in a year, so no, I don't think so."

"Look, I know you and your mom—"

"At least Mom's been here. That's more than you can say." Prestyn picks up her phone again as her father's smile vanishes. He bows his head and rests it on his clasped hands, like he's lost in thought, or praying.

Mr. Donaldson starts again more softly. "You're right. And I should be honest with you. I came in for a reason." He picks up the brochure next to him and starts to fiddle with it. "I . . . I thought you might want to take a look at this," he says. "It's from the Stonebury School."

The Stonebury School!

She takes it and her eyes widen. She's as shocked as Donnybrooke. "Omigod! You want to send me away! Have you even told Mom?"

Mr. Donaldson flushes and runs his fingers through his hair. "Of course. We've talked. And it's not about sending you away. Not at all," he says. "It's just that these are hard years, and Stonebury could make them easier. We were planning on looking at it for high school anyway."

"Excuse me, did you say 'easier'? Because you always talk about how strict it was. How there were a million rules. How you could get detention for the littlest thing." She claps her hand on her head. "Omigod, I can't even have this conversation." She gets to her feet and stomps to the door.

"Wait! Please!"

"Don't even try to tell me how awesome it was." Her hand is clenching the doorknob.

"I won't. It was strict. It absolutely was. But strict because they care enough to hold you accountable, even if it might be less work to look the other way. The standards are high because they believe in you. They know there's more to you than who you are at your worst." It's clear Prestyn is listening now as her grip on the knob loosens. Her father is clutching the brochure with both hands. He starts to wring it. "When I was your age, Pressie, there wasn't a line I wouldn't cross. What you did—"

"I told you. It was an accident," says Prestyn.

Mr. Donaldson talks right over her. "C'mon, Prestyn. We both know better."

"I thought you didn't want me to get in trouble. Isn't that why you made sure I could go back to Castleton?"

"That was my first instinct, but I'm not sure it was the right one. Look, the world is so much bigger than Coreville. I think it's time for you to be in a place where everyone hasn't known you since first grade. Where you're starting over with kids from all over the country, the world even. And with adults who'll give you structure and boundaries and even a kind of family."

"I can't believe you don't want me here." She tugs a loose thread on her sweater but doesn't seem to notice it unraveling.

"Are you kidding? I'll miss you like crazy if you go. But I'm up there at least once a month for board meetings, more if there's special events. Heck, sometimes I think I spend more time up there than here." He chuckles, but Prestyn does not. He glances back down at the brochure, now crumpled, and tries to press it flat between his hands. "Look, I know everyone thinks I'm a dork for being so into my high school. But it's not because I want to be quarterback of the football team again. It's because those people believed in me at a time when I needed a lot of work. They helped me be my best. I think they could do the same for you."

His words hang in the round room. It's the most he's said to Prestyn in one sitting in the last year. And while it's undoubtedly positive that he's showing an interest in her again, why isn't he having a heart-to-heart about how much better they can all do here in Donnybrooke instead of some school hundreds of miles away? Surely Mr. Donaldson could keep the conversation closer to home. Prestyn seems to agree. She flops on her bed and buries her face in a pillow. The white one Mrs. Donaldson told her not to stain.

"Just think about it," Mr. Donaldson says. He smooths out the brochure one last time and leaves it on her nightstand.

Don't leave me alone, Donnybrooke wants to tell her. *Please, my princess, there's no place like home.*

For the next few days, Mr. Donaldson steers clear of Prestyn's turret, and Donnybrooke breathes a sigh of relief. It's time to get on with life and forget all that Stonebury silliness. Though Prestyn might not quite understand that. The Stonebury brochure stays on her nightstand, and the Stonebury home page stays up on her phone. She looks at it every night.

And then it happens: Mr. Donaldson knocks on her door, and this time, she lets him in with a small smile. Then she sits on her bed and curls her toes deep into her soft pink shag rug. They certainly don't have *those* in boarding school.

"I don't know," she finally says.

"I understand. In some ways, it would be so much easier to let everything just stay how it' s been . . . The thing is, I think we can all do better."

Of course they can. That's Donnybrooke's whole point.

"But I don't think we will unless we make some real changes. So, let me put it to you another way: Do you want to stay here?"

She does. She must. Donnybrooke is the only home she remembers.

Prestyn's eyes scan her room's round wall and drift up the

slant of the turret, settling on the peak. They rest there. It's the longest she's looked at it since that very first time with Asha when everything was new.

Stay, my princess, stay, Donnybrooke tries to tell her. *Please just give me one more chance.*

Prestyn meets her father's eyes.

And shakes her head no.

Sam

The pollen is the worst thing Sam has encountered all week. The glaze of it on the sidewalk is so thick as he walks home from Our Lady of Mercy that for the first time all year, Sam finds himself hoping that the gray clouds in the distance roll this way.

He runs into the mail carrier at his front door. She hands him the usual stack of clothing catalogues and coupon books. Most of it Sam's mom will toss when she gets home, but if it's addressed to her, he leaves it for her. His only exception is for Castleton Academy fundraising requests. Those go straight to recycling.

In today's mix of junk mail is a small mint-green envelope. Addressed to Sam Moss. The only mail he ever gets is birthday cards from his grandmothers, and his birthday isn't for months. And this handwriting isn't like either grandma's. It's round and neat, even neater than Sam's, and his first thought is of Prestyn.

He hasn't talked to her since that night.

He hasn't been back to Castleton and he doesn't want to go back to Castleton, but he would like to see Prestyn one more time. Just to ask her why. When he talks to his psychologist, Dr. Ernesto, about what happened, he says that it wasn't about Sam. But still, it would be nice to hear that from Prestyn herself.

He flips the envelope over. The return address—without a name—is printed in capital letters on the back. 8705 Larksong Lane. It's not Prestyn's house. Or Asha's.

He opens it. The stationery has pressed flowers in it and feels more like cloth than paper.

Dear Sam, it starts in neat silver ink.

> *I know this apology is very late, but all the same I want to say I'm sorry for how I treated you. It was so wrong. I am still not exactly sure why I went along with Prestyn. At the time, I couldn't imagine standing up to her. Now I can't imagine why I didn't. I don't want to be the kind of person who doesn't know right from wrong, or, even worse, does know, but isn't brave enough to act on it.*
>
> *I hope you are happy at your new school and have lots of friends who like you for who you are. Also, thank you for all your work on the Medieval Life*

project. Not just for getting us an A, but for teaching me that lots of people in the Middle Ages knew the earth was round, the importance of building a well inside the walls, and what a real castle looked like— which is nothing like Donnybrooke. All your facts were super interesting!

Sincerely,

Tessa Ferrer

Sam's throat is tight. The first time he reads the letter, it brings him back to Donnybrooke and Castleton and being too cold and being called Miracle Boy, and that feeling that he was always doing something wrong. But once he thinks about it more, he realizes that Tessa is saying just the opposite, that none of this was his fault. And he likes that she appreciated all his Medieval Life facts. He didn't even know she was paying attention. He reads the letter again and again. The only thing that would make it better is if it were from Prestyn.

He decides to hide it in his closet between his planetarium umbrella and the box of souvenirs from his Kennedy Space Center trip. He wants that letter just for himself. Even when it's out of sight, it stays on his mind, and he walks a little lighter, like there's a bit less gravity to pull him down.

That weekend, Sam kills the At-tick Fana-tick for the fourth time ever. He figured out how last month—the trick is squeezing fine-point tweezers to its head—and now he makes mistakes on purpose just for the fight. Of course he makes sure he has a master bathroom first, because that's where you find the tweezers, and he doesn't bother with matches, because it's nearly impossible to grasp them and the tweezers at the same time. This is one monster that requires a firm grip.

As soon as Sam drops the Fana-tick out a window, confetti and streamers fall from the ceiling, he gets his choice of finished wings to add on to his house, and all of his Zombie-Selves immediately become new lives for him to use. It's pretty awesome. The only way it would be cooler is if the whole thing were in outer space. Not that Asha would agree. At least he doesn't think she would.

They haven't talked since she rescued him. It's not that he doesn't want to; it's just that every time he thinks about it, every time his mom or dad suggests it, he gets jittery all over. What would he even say?

He puts down his phone and goes to his closet. As he takes the planetarium umbrella out, Tessa's apology letter flutters to the ground. He reads it one more time. The silver of its ink is just like the silver of the tweezers he used on the At-tick Fana-tick.

Asha still probably doesn't know how to kill it.

Sam finds Asha sitting in the Japanese maple in her front yard. The leaves are in bloom, green turning to red, and from his angle, a cluster of branches hides her face.

"Hi, Asha," he says to her sandals. This conversation might be easier if he can just talk to her feet.

The tree rustles a little like there are squirrels in it, but she doesn't come down.

"Thank you for helping me when I was at Donnybrooke," he says. It's the sentence he's practiced his whole way over here.

Asha's branch bounces a bit.

And suddenly there's so much more Sam wants to say while she's still up there and he doesn't have to look at her. "I'm sorry that I wasn't a good friend. And I'm sorry I asked you to save me at Donnybrooke when it's such a scary place. And if you want I can show you how to kill the At-tick Fana-tick."

Asha is on the ground before he even gets out the monster's name. "They're moving," she says. "So maybe it won't be so scary anymore."

"Who's moving?"

"The Donaldsons. There's an open house today. Didn't you know?"

He didn't. He feels the news right in his chest. It doesn't seem fair that Prestyn can leave without saying sorry first. But at least

Sam will no longer be worried about running into her at the orthodontist or Coreville Farmcart or anywhere else. It's not the same as a real apology. He'd rather have that. But breathing space is still worth something.

"Do you want me to show you?" says Sam. "You just need tweezers."

"Tweezers?"

"To kill the At-tick Fana-tick."

Asha shakes her head. "I play a different game now."

"What?" That's impossible. Asha loves Househaunt.

"I play House. Without the Haunt."

"Huh? I've never heard of that."

"Of course not. I'm making it myself in coding class so I can just do the parts I like. Which is building the house without all the creepy monsters." She jumps with her arms up and catches a branch. She swings a few times before landing on her feet. "You could do it, except make Haunt with all monsters and no architecture."

"Or I could finally make Spacehaunt," says Sam. This conversation reminds him of all their time in the car to and from Ms. Summer's when they would talk and laugh and ignore each other. They were so little then.

"I take the class on Thursdays at Coreville Community Center," says Asha. "You could do it, too."

"I can't," says Sam. "I see a therapist on Thursdays. Dr. Ernesto." No one else knows that except his parents. Usually he leaves the office fast with his head down, like he's a spy or something. Even the kids he likes at school have no idea.

Asha grabs the branch again and swings. "Is he nice? I see Dr. Wells and she's super nice. She has the best candy in the waiting area, too."

"He is nice," says Sam. "And we talk about stuff that helps me, like how to trust myself more. It's just that I'd thought I was done working on things."

Asha drops to her feet and stands next to him. "But everyone has to work on things. Whether or not they have appointments. Look at Pre— you-know-who."

Yes, like Prestyn. But really all of the kids from Castleton. And his new school, Our Lady of Mercy. And Sullivan Middle School. Everywhere, really. Everyone has something. It's easy to forget that sometimes.

"You can take the coding class on Saturdays, too," says Asha.

"Really?" says Sam. "Can I play your new game?"

To his surprise, Asha shakes her head. "Not now. My friend is about to come over."

"Maybe another time?"

"Maybe."

"I'll text you," he says, and jogs off.

Once he crosses Coreville Avenue, he picks up his pace. Maybe he will ask his mom about that coding class. Maybe that will be one more thing he loves, along with running and space and killing monsters. He might even be really good at it.

But for right now, with the sun on his back and his breath coming steady, this day is enough and he is enough.

And that, by itself, feels like a miracle.

Asha

Asha and Joanna arrive at the Donnybrooke open house at 12:58, two minutes before it officially starts. Kelsey Britt, "real estate agent extraordinaire" according to her ads, is straightening out a cherry blossom wreath on the front door. She greets the girls with a once-over, then gives them a practiced smile and says, "There's cookies and information about the house in the sunroom. And if you like it, please tell your parents. We're open until four."

"My mom already knows," says Asha. In fact, her mom was the one who told her that Donnybrooke was for sale and that the Donaldsons wouldn't be at the open house so she could explore as much as she wanted. Even so, Asha holds her breath as she walks through the front door, bracing herself for, if not the Donaldsons, the eagle-and-fish painting at least.

But it's gone. In its place is a large abstract painting, with smears and drips of white and blue, that reminds Asha of someplace vast and calming like the ocean or the sky. It's very pretty, but so not Donnybrooke. Asha almost wonders if she's still qualified to give the tour she promised Joanna.

But the rest of the first level is more or less as she remembered except that the furniture in the living room has been rearranged and, of course, the disco ball from the party is gone. Joanna takes a few pictures as they make their way to the sunroom for cookies. Then they explore the back of the house all the way to the spiral staircase. Joanna sits and looks up and down.

"It's like being in a snail shell," she says.

"Exactly!"

"Let's go down and explore."

Asha's stomach twists at the thought of being back in the basement. It's the one place she won't go. That and the elevator. "I don't want to. But you can."

"OK, I'll meet you upstairs," says Joanna, taking off with the agility that's made her so tough on the volleyball court.

Asha stands on the threshold between the stairs and the main floor, where she first watched the kids dancing at Prestyn's party. She'd been jealous of how the girls hung off one another like they were all one big organism. But now she knows there are other ways to not feel alone.

She retreats to the staircase and goes up. She's headed to the room with the roof deck stairs. This time, instead of following the noise, she can follow the smell, the not-so-faint odor of fresh paint. The stairs are down, and Asha tests her weight on the first one. It holds her solidly, and she runs up to the roof.

Outside, she instinctively looks up to the weather vane, but of course it's not there. It still makes Asha sad to think of it in a landfill. She looks down on the town of Coreville, and the view is so precisely how she imagined that it's hard to believe she's only been here that one quick time when she was six. She spots her house and Sullivan Middle School and Joanna's apartment building and the cars along Coreville Avenue, but everything looks smaller, toylike, as if she's in a plane coming down for landing. The trees are the only things that truly hold their own.

Asha leans against a large planter. Even though it's spring, nothing is growing in it now. But it's still decorative, filled with small, smooth multicolored pebbles. Asha takes a handful and runs them through her fingers. They patter down like raindrops. She does it again, and then again, and then—she sees it: two black metal points, the tips of a shallow V, protruding from within the planter. That space, that angle. Her heart pounds.

She wiggles it hard, then gently, then hard. Tail, then fins, then head—her breath quickens with each one—and then the whole fish comes loose. The Donnybrooke fish! She never thought she'd see it again, let alone touch it, but here it is! She holds it up by the tail, careful to avoid the jagged spot where it broke off from the rest of the weather vane. Her wrist wobbles slightly. It's heavier than she expected.

She studies its face—its mouth is a flat line. She'd always wondered if it was supposed to feel more sad or more scared being so close to that eagle, but this fish is neither. It's serious. Like it's on a mission to save itself. Like it believes escape is possible. Like it doesn't have time to worry about the odds. And now it's free.

Asha looks back up at the spot where the weather vane was. It's gone now, gone for good. Just like the Donaldsons. The fish outlasted them all. But there's no reason for it to stay here any longer. She sticks it, headfirst, into her baggy shorts pocket. It only half fits, but her loose sweatshirt covers the rest. She presses her arm to her side to hold it steady and let it make one last getaway.

By the time Asha goes back inside Donnybrooke, the house is buzzing with the low murmur of visitors. She passes younger couples and older neighbors whispering their thoughts to one another in library voices as she searches the top floor for Joanna. Asha finds her alone in Prestyn's room.

"You're right," says Joanna. "It's prettier inside than out."

Asha's eyes drift up to the turret, just as perfect and pointed as ever. She gets a twinge in her throat as she remembers how much she used to love it.

"But even so," says Joanna, "I can't imagine living here. It doesn't feel like a home."

It doesn't to Asha either anymore, and she feels bad for this house that's trying so, so hard. "I think it still could, though. One day."

She and Joanna wander out to the atrium balcony and look down on all the people who have come. They move in different directions, but purposefully, like ants in a colony. Asha hopes there's someone down there who appreciates Donnybrooke with all of its quirks, who understands what it might be. Someone who loves it the way she once did.

Now that would make it a truly lucky home.

10001 Hunt Place

Seeking a Family

So, if you've never been shown at an open house, here's what you need to know:

It's like hosting a party, but twice as nerve-racking. The guests are largely strangers, there isn't a room that's off-limits, and there's not an hors d'oeuvre in sight (though the meticulous Ms. Britt did put out a plate of assorted Coreville Farmcart tea cookies). Ms. Britt makes sure you look your "very, very best" whether you want her to or not. To be fair, she's not all bad. She was the driving force behind getting the roof deck and its stairs fixed. She also had the D&B crest removed from the front gates, which was quite a change at first, but the house is admittedly lighter without it.

The ramblers and split-levels down the street have all had their own open houses, and they share tips, too. Try to relax.

Don't stress about the nosy neighbors. Look for the families who linger. Even the trees are being cooperative today, standing by graciously with their foliage in full bloom.

Since the moment the doors officially opened, there's been a steady stream of couples and neighbors. They peer into the bathrooms and closets, they whisper about fixtures and finishes, but in the end, they come, and then they go. Except for one family. They've stayed longer than any other.

They have three children, and the middle one, a boy, has found Prestyn's old room. He is lying on the polished wood floor, admiring the turret in a way that it hasn't been admired since the very first party here. He's bigger than Asha was when she first visited, but not by much.

The grown-ups, Ms. Britt especially, appear glad not to have him underfoot. His first move upon entering the sunroom was to turn on the ceiling fan, which not only caused the flyers to go flying but also tore the paper lanterns Ms. Britt had so carefully hung. Although, really, any house could have told you those lanterns were not the right look for that room. Donnybrooke, for one, breathed a sigh of relief when she was forced to take them down, even if the child's parents were most apologetic.

Now the entire family is wandering and re-wandering in and out of rooms. The boy's older sister is going up the spiral

staircase for the second time just as Asha and her new friend are going down.

"Isn't this house cool?" says Asha as they pass. "I bet you would love living here."

She's always been a delightful girl, that one.

Something about the boy in Prestyn's room is reminiscent of Asha. He cares about how this house was made, what holds it together, what makes it tick. He might even love it. "Isaiah! What are you doing on the floor?" says his mom when she finds him. The toddler in her arms squirms out. To be honest, this little one may be a cause for concern. He's drooled quite a bit. When he reaches his big brother, he drops both hands on his chest and giggles.

Oh! That sound!

The boy, Isaiah, rubs the toddler's fuzzy head, but doesn't take his eyes off the turret. The toddler looks up, too, and giggles again.

Imagine hearing that every day. Really it's its own music.

The older girl wanders in with her dad behind her. First she takes in the shape of the room, and then her family.

"I think this should be Isaiah's room," she says.

Her dad laughs. "You've already got us buying this house, Elise."

"I love it, Dad! It's got personality."

Together, the five of them, each with their own smile, stare up to the tip of the turret. Donnybrooke wants them to stay. Wants to witness their birthdays and their holidays. To lull them to sleep with the rain on the roof and decorate their windows with icicles. To warm them and cool them. To care for them. To love them. To shelter them.

It's like Asha said. It still can be a home.

Perhaps more than it's ever been before.

Acknowledgments

So many people have encouraged me, taught me, and helped me with this book, I could write another novel just to thank everyone. (Well, it might not have much of a plot, but it would hit the word count.) Even in this group, though, there are standouts.

Molly Ker Hawn, the very best agent there is. A mansion-load of thanks for your wisdom, your enthusiasm, your brilliance, and your kindness. I'm so lucky to have you in my corner.

Susan Van Metre, my thoughtful, precise, and patient editor: Working with you has been an absolute joy. Thank you for giving this book—and me—such a warm and welcoming home.

I'm grateful to the excellent team at Walker Books US/ Candlewick, including Maggie Deslaurier, Mary Beth Constant, Lana Barnes, Emily Quill, Karen Walsh, Sawako Shirota, and

Lindsay Warren. Nicole Miles and Maya Tatsukawa, I love how you brought this story to life with your amazing cover and book design. Thank you also to Denise Johnstone-Burt and the Walker UK team for your support.

Thank you to Sarah Kapit for serving as a sensitivity reader on this book. It is so much better for your nuance and insight. Any shortcomings are my own. Also, thank you for your support of my story, your advocacy, and the terrific books you write.

Thank you to Alicia Carbaugh, Mare Hagerty, and Alison Green Myers for valuable comments on early drafts of this novel, and to Maria Frazer, Arielle Vishny, and Angele McQuade for advice that helped me bring this book into the world. And thank you to all my writer friends for being there for me through the ups and downs. I'm so glad to be on this journey with you.

I attended two Highlights Foundation workshops where excerpts of this novel were reviewed. I'm grateful to the leaders and participants for their feedback, with particular thanks to Elizabeth Schoenfeld, who critiqued the whole novel afterward.

The book *Castle* by David Macaulay was a fascinating read and helped me articulate the differences between a real castle and Donnybrooke. I highly recommend it.

Thank you to my longtime friends who cheered me on as I wrote this book and have filled my life with so much love. You know who you are.

Janet Holden and the Maniases, I'm so glad I'm a part of your family and so appreciative of your encouragement.

Thank you to my sister, Veena Trehan, for never doubting I could do this and for making me laugh the way no one else can.

Thank you to my parents, Ranvir and Adarsh Trehan, for a lifetime of boundless love, support, and faith in me.

Curran and Maya, you bring immeasurable joy to my life. This story would not exist without you. So much love to you both.

And finally, to Curt, the love of my life and partner in all things: How did I get so lucky?

About the Author

Meera Trehan grew up in Virginia, just outside Washington, DC. After attending the University of Virginia and Stanford Law School, she practiced law for more than a decade before turning to creative writing. She lives in Maryland with her family.